Could a chance encounter be the start of a new life for Brenda Sparks?

A tingle of excitement touched Brenda. A woman would be crazy not to want to work for this gorgeous man! As Brenda realized where her thoughts were taking her, she stiffened; she tensed. Pain clutched at her. She must be crazy. This pull of attraction had to be stifled at once. A relationship with any man was no longer possible for her.

She opened her mouth to say that she could not work for him but it snapped shut and she swallowed quickly as she remembered just how desperate she was for a job. And then another thought struck her: *Was this God's provision?* There were less than three weeks before Jack's wedding and she would have to get out of this flat if she couldn't afford to take over the very modest rental costs.

The tall man continued to silently study the expressions that flickered across her face. Suddenly he thrust out his hand. "Look, let's start again. Hello, Miss Sparks, my name's Blake Warwyck and I desperately need help."

MARY HAWKINS lives in Australia with her husband; they have three grown children. Her first inspirational novel, *Search for Tomorrow*, was voted the second most favorite contemporary by **Heartsong Presents** readers.

Books by Mary Hawkins

HEARTSONG PRESENTS

HP 42—Search for Tomorrow

Damaged Dreams

Mary Hawkins

Heartsong Presents

For my dear mum, Gladys Pedler,
who first started praying for me before I was born.

I love to hear from my readers! You may write to me at the
following address:

> **Mary Hawkins**
> **Author Relations**
> **P.O. Box 719**
> **Uhrichsville, OH 44683**

ISBN 1-55748-588-7

DAMAGED DREAMS

one

"I really am sorry, Miss Sparks." The woman had moved from behind the receptionist's desk.

Her hesitant voice faded away as Brenda just kept stomping out of the doctor's waiting room with her back straight and her head up. No way would she let that woman see how upset she was, thought Brenda. She blinked rapidly to stop the second tear from trickling down her face.

"Watch out, young lady!" An exasperated male voice rapped out the words. Two large hands grasped her above the elbows as she blindly swung around the corner of the corridor.

"Watch out yourself!" she heard herself snap back as she tried to tug her arms free.

The supporting hands were abruptly withdrawn. With horror she felt herself start to topple over and she knew immediately what had happened. Somehow her left foot was not placed flat on the ground as she had been repeatedly trained to do.

Frantically, she reached out for support and found herself holding onto the strong arm she had just vigorously rejected. Another arm grabbed for her waist and pulled her against him to prevent her falling. Thankfully, she leaned her full weight into the firm body. Her face pressed harder into a broad shoulder and both her hands desperately clung to him as she struggled to move her right leg. Then she balanced awkwardly on that leg so she could lift her left foot to its correct position.

Suddenly she was very conscious of leaning against muscles that had tensed to take her full weight. When she moved her head from that supporting shoulder and tentatively started to distribute her weight evenly on both legs, her face brushed against his chin and the faintest whiff of after shave drifted toward her. Slowly she straightened up. *Would these legs never stop letting her down?* she thought. As she regained her balance, she closed her eyes tightly for a moment.

Her eyes flew open. "I'm. . .I'm so sorry," she gasped. She was a very tall girl but, as she straightened to her full height, the pair of dark brown eyes were still a few inches above her own. The wide forehead above the thin black eyebrows was creased into a frown. Brenda's dazed eyes traveled farther to the black hair that formed a peak in the middle of that forehead and then was swept back over a well-shaped head.

Vaguely, she felt that she had seen that strong face before somewhere. Even the cleft in that firm jaw seemed familiar.

"Are you all right?" he asked. The voice was slow and filled with concern. It sounded very North American to her Australian ears.

With dismay, Brenda realized that both his hands were still gripping her at the waist and that their bodies were still far too close. "Yes, of course," she answered.

Her voice sounded all wrong and she swallowed rapidly to clear her throat. She opened her mouth to repeat the words but was suddenly speechless as he took one of his hands from her waist, placed a finger beneath her eye, and then brushed it across her cheek. The moisture on the tip of his finger was held up for her inspection. She had not even realized that more than that second tear had trickled

from her eyes. One of those dark eyebrows flew up in unbelief.

"Is everything all right, Miss Sparks?"

At the sound of the woman's voice behind them, the dark
eyes lifted from Brenda's misty ones and looked over her
shoulder. The frown disappeared as his attractive face was
transformed by a dazzling smile.

"Blake! Oh, Blake, you're back!"

Suddenly his warmth and support were gone. For a fleeting moment, Brenda felt bereft as the stranger stepped back
from her and was then enveloped in the clinging arms of
the beautiful blond from the doctor's office. Before Brenda's
startled gaze, he was soundly kissed. And he was returning that cuddle just as enthusiastically, she thought sourly.

She turned away and began to walk, more carefully this
time, down the hallway toward the row of lifts.* After only
a few paces, she felt a light touch on her shoulder.

"Are you sure you're all right?" he asked.

She paused, feeling absurdly pleased that he had followed her. "Yes, I'm fine. Truly."

"Perhaps if you chose not to wear such a long, loose
skirt, you would be much easier on the people you bump
into." Condemning eyes were looking down her body at
the soft material that flowed around her legs until it just
touched the floor.

"It's not a skirt, it's a culotte," she blurted out defensively.

Then she went rigid. Had he noticed her leg? Her eyes
flew to his, looking for the usual dreaded sympathy or
curiosity. For a moment, her eyes seemed to lock with his.
The brown eyes seemed to darken until they were almost
black, searching to her very soul. As she remained silent, a
puzzled look replaced the intensity of his gaze.

*Elevators

"Well, if you're sure. . .," he began doubtfully and then he suddenly stiffened as she remained silent. A cool look replaced the question in his eyes. "Perhaps you had just better be more careful and look where you're going." The words were unexpectedly crisp and a little scornful.

The anger and hurt that had still been bubbling deep within her suddenly surfaced. She raised her chin. "Be more careful yourself!" she snapped. She was conscious of his eyes on her as she moved away from him toward the lift.

"Oh, Blake, do come and tell me what's been happening." The woman's voice sounded impatient.

Brenda jabbed at the button for the lift. The doors slid open immediately and she held her culottes up as she stepped forward. As the lift doors slid shut, she caught a final glimpse of him. He was still staring after her, the blond hanging onto his arm.

Just as well all the obstetrician's patients had gone for the day or some might have had their babies on the spot if those two indulged in any more fond "hello" sessions, she thought nastily and then immediately felt ashamed. In her entire life, she had never spoken so rudely to a stranger. And the way he held another woman was certainly none of her business.

She closed her eyes tightly. *Well, God, I blew that one!* she thought a little defiantly. *I hope You realized it was definitely the last straw.* Then she stilled. A couple more tears slid down her cheeks. This time they were more for her own behavior than for what had happened.

That man really had been good holding her until she had regained her balance. Although she had lost a lot of weight this past year, she knew she was no featherweight. It wasn't very often she met a man so much taller than herself. He must have been well over six feet, and he had certainly fielded her very competently, she decided rather reluctantly.

The lift doors slid open. She hastily brushed away the tears and then sighed as she quickly glanced at her watch before moving slowly out into the foyer of the building.

It was no good trying to catch the next bus. It would be long gone by the time she reached the stop and there would be at least another half-hour to wait for the next one. But hopefully there would be a seat to sit on. Still shaken by the near fall and her yielding to the anger and frustration deep within, she very carefully negotiated her way through the busy Newcastle city center mall.

Her eyes automatically avoided eye contact with any of the passers-by. It had proven to be an effective tool to miss the looks that made her hurt deep inside. All her prayers to date hadn't completely stopped that and today she was feeling particularly vulnerable. She still hated the way curious eyes swept down her long culotte, obviously wondering why she limped so badly. At least today she did not have her walking stick for them to gawk at as well. But if she had, she might not have made such a fool of herself in front of one of the most handsome men she had ever seen.

She wondered if she really had seen him before somewhere. As a nurse she had met so many people over the years that occasionally she did meet someone whom she couldn't place. But, of course, for two years she had been so much in love with Robert, that she had rarely noticed other men.

Her lips tightened into the disciplined straight line that had become only too familiar during the last few months. She deliberately swung her thoughts away from the past and back to the present. What on earth was she going to do if she couldn't find a job, and soon?

That woman in the doctor's office had seemed genuinely

sorry that they had not been able to reach her to tell her that they no longer needed a part-time nurse receptionist. It had been the last straw after a very frustrating and humiliating day of fruitless appointments.

The hot hours had seemed endless since Brenda had left the flat.* A wave of exhaustion swept over her when she at last found herself hanging onto the strap in the crowded aisle of the bus. She had not realized it was so close to the peak hour rush. Many times in the past week, she had gamely climbed in and out of buses but, up until today, she had always been able to avoid them when they might be crowded. The bus lurched around a corner and she grabbed for the back of the seat near her. She missed and grabbed a young man's shoulder instead. He turned and glared at her.

"Sorry. My legs are still recovering from a car accident." Not really a lie, she consoled herself as she looked sadly at him. To her satisfaction, he blushed faintly, and than stood up and gestured for her to sit down.

"Oh, thank you so much," she said with immense relief, as she awkwardly maneuvered herself into the vacant seat. Her best hundred-watt smile was beamed up at him after she had settled and, to her secret delight, he blushed scarlet and then moved farther toward the back of the bus.

Before leaning back into the seat, she tried to position her left leg more comfortably. Perhaps after all, she was going to have to give up any idea of using her long years of training to get some job where it would be used even a little.

"I'm sorry, Sister Sparks," the Director of Nursing at the Royal Hospital had said frankly, although sympathetically. "Unfortunately, nurses in the majority of positions, especially for which you are eligible, need two strong legs

—————
*Apartment

and feet to even begin to cope with the pressures of their work. I can only keep you in mind if something comes up."

And that could take a very long time indeed, Brenda thought gloomily. The position at that private pathology department might have been okay if only there had been a lift in the building. Perhaps there would be a job like that in another department in one of the suburbs. Transport would then more than likely be her biggest problem. *And I've been praying so hard about it all! God has brought me this far,* she reminded herself. *Surely He wouldn't let me down now.*

She sighed again and closed her eyes. Immediately the image of dark brown eyes in a strong face intruded. Her eyes flew open as she frowned. She still had a vague feeling that she had seen him before somewhere. And why would he be visiting an obstetrical surgery? Undoubtedly to see his blond friend, she found herself thinking a little wistfully.

Usually the bus took only fifteen minutes to reach her street, but today it was so crowded it seemed to take forever. At last Brenda recognized a landmark and reached up to press the stop button.

The large bus slid to a smooth halt and the driver waited patiently for Brenda to awkwardly push her way through the few passengers still standing.

"Thank you," she murmured politely, as she carefully and painfully lowered her two aching legs down the high steps and out onto the grassy footpath.

The folding doors clicked shut behind her and the bus had moved away before she stepped onto the strip of cement path. She looked up and gave a gasp of dismay.

"Hey! Come back, it's the wrong stop!" she yelled foolishly, as the bus disappeared down the tree-lined street.

The peak hour bus must have followed a different route. Instead of just needing to cross the road, she was at least a block away from home.

The tears were very near again as she made her way to the bus stop seat and eased herself carefully onto it. Suddenly she even felt too down to pray about this fix. Besides, by now God must be sick to death of all her needs today!

She saw a small yellow car coming toward her and fervently wished it could have been a taxi. To her surprise, it suddenly screeched to a stop beside her. There was a toot on the horn and then a familiar face was grinning at her over the roof. "Need a lift, lady?"

"Oh, Doug," she sighed with relief, "Never did a lady need a lift more." *In more ways than one,* she added grimly to herself. "But what a comedown." She waved at the car as the stockily built teenager joined her. "What happened to your monster?"

"Monster? How dare you call my beautiful Yamaha motorbike a monster! I don't think the lady needs a lift after all." His huge grin negated the threat of his words. He held out his two hands toward her. She grasped them tightly and levered herself up. "Unfortunately, even the best sometimes needs attention. She's getting a new tire but it wasn't ready by the time I had to leave for training, so me mate loaned me this car. Now, this is a monstrosity!"

He had kept talking as he helped her over to the car. She thankfully let him lift her left leg in for her before he slammed the door and moved around to the driver's seat. He revved the motor before taking a quick look behind and, swinging around in a U-turn, narrowly missed a brown station wagon that must have come around the corner at the same time.

"Doug!" Brenda exclaimed in fright.

"Oops! Sorry," he drawled, glancing in the rear vision mirror.

"It shouldn't be me you're apologizing to," she muttered.

It only took a few seconds to reach the flat. There was a much more sedate U-turn, but a screech of brakes as they pulled up outside the door. Brenda noted that the station wagon was also pulling to a stop across the street. Poor driver was still feeling shellshocked, she thought as Doug helped her out and escorted her to the gateway opening onto the small front yard.

Never had she been more thankful that there were only a few steps up to her foster brother Jack's flat. She clung to the sturdy new rail that had been constructed especially for her and hauled herself slowly up the steps. At the top, she turned to thank Doug, to see him with his hand out for the key.

"Don't make yourself any later for your training session," she said to him gratefully. "I'll be okay now."

He cocked his head to one side and studied her face. "Are you sure you'll be right by yourself? You look pretty pale to me. Pretty, but pale!"

She smiled gently at him. "It has been another rough day but I'll be fine after I've had a rest. Thank you for being such a dear." She reached over and gave him a big hug and kissed him on the cheek.

"Wow!" he stammered. Color lightly stained the skin under his youthful, unshaven beard. "You're some woman, Brenda." He gave her a quick kiss on the lips. "And I guess your God'll look out for you as you're always tellin' me He does." He gave her a cheeky grin before turning away.

She watched him thoughtfully as he ran back down the

steps. There had been a few opportunities to talk to the young man about her faith. Perhaps some words had penetrated his diffident attitude to God after all. She took a deep breath before finding her key and entering the cool house.

Since she had moved here, Doug had been a wonderful help to her. At first she had been very wary of the young men who shared the rent on the house next door. She still didn't like the other two, but a rapport had sprung up between her and the seventeen-year-old Doug Stewart. There had been something about him that had reminded her of that other young boy she had met so briefly nearly twelve months ago.

But that was part of the memories she dared not dwell on, especially after such a disastrous day. Wearily, she moved into the bathroom and freshened herself with a quick wash. With disgust she noted that her hair had been partly dislodged from where she had secured it at the back of her head in a loose roll. It had probably happened when she had been held so tightly against that beautifully muscled body.

I wonder what he does to keep fit, she mused as she shook her thick, dark, rusty brown hair free and picked up a brush. She smiled at herself in the mirror. The smile turned to a chuckle. He would need to keep fit if he went around fielding two women in such a short space of time every day. I wonder if she felt as warmed as I did. A kiss from those lips could probably start a brush fire.

The hazel eyes staring back at her in the mirror suddenly went wide with dismay. Anyone would think she had been jealous of that kiss! She groaned. It had really been a dreadful day if she was so tired that her thoughts went haywire like this!

Decisively, she went out to the small kitchen and plugged in the electric kettle. Boy, did she need something to eat— and to take her mind off that near fall. Until she had some nourishment in her, she dared not sit down and relax because she knew the effort to get up again would be too much. The boiling water had just been poured into her coffee mug when there was a couple of sharp knocks on the door.

A little apprehensively, she put down the mug and made her way slowly across the room. One of the men next door had come over a few times during the past week on some flimsy excuse to borrow something, and his attitude had started to worry her. She knew that Doug was out, and no one else had ever come here when Jack was away for any length of time.

She opened the door and then gasped. It was the stranger she had collided with in town earlier. That black hair looked as though he had combed it back with his fingers several times since he had held her so tightly with those strong hands, she thought in a daze. He surely was tall! Her eyes flickered over the white shirt and the somber black and gray tie, down the long legs encased by sharply creased black trousers. When she raised her eyes to his face again, she found he was also busy studying her curves. By the glint of admiration on his face, he, too, liked what he saw!

"What. . .what are you doing here?" she asked.

"Doctor Harrison gave me your address," he answered.

A very attractive pair of lips curved into an amused smile as she gaped at him. The cleft in his chin almost disappeared but two elusive dimples peeped at her from his cheeks. *My, my,* she thought again, *he's even more attractive than I realized before.* The smile became a big grin and his eyes twinkled beguilingly at her.

"I thought that our meeting was a little back to front. I usually embrace beautiful women after we have been introduced, not when they throw themselves into my arms as soon as they see me."

His voice was deep and so filled with amusement that she found an answering well of laughter bubbling up from some deep spring within her. "And I'll have you know, I only throw myself into a man's arms at no less than the second meeting," she heard herself flash back. Then one hand flew to her mouth, and she stared at him with horror, as she realized what she had said.

He threw back his head and laughed with delight. "Good, you've got a sense of humor."

Then he sobered quickly, the light fading from his eyes. He stared at her intently for a moment and, when the laughter had fled, his eyes seemed much darker. For one fanciful moment, she wondered if he was once again trying to see into her very soul.

"You might need that sense of humour, if you—" He broke off and a lean hand did rake through his black hair. "Look, I know this is unusual, but Julie said she thought it was a real blow to you when you found out the job as nurse was no longer available and I am desperate enough to wonder if you would consider working for me."

two

A tingle of excitement touched Brenda. A woman would be crazy not to want to work for this gorgeous man! As Brenda realized where her thoughts were taking her, she stiffened; she tensed. Pain clutched at her. She must be crazy. This pull of attraction had to be stifled at once. A relationship with any man was no longer possible for her.

She opened her mouth to say that she could not work for him but it snapped shut and she swallowed quickly as she remembered just how desperate she was for a job. And then another thought struck her: *Was this God's provision?* There were less than three weeks before Jack's wedding and she would have to get out of this flat if she couldn't afford to take over the very modest rental costs.

The tall man continued to silently study the expressions that flickered across her face. Suddenly he thrust out his hand. "Look, let's start again. Hello, Miss Sparks, my name's Blake Warwyck and I desperately need help."

Brenda found her own hand formally being shaken and then politely dropped. Unconsciously she rubbed her hand down her side as though it had been stung. His eyes followed the movement and, when they looked back at her face, she felt heat suddenly touch her cheeks.

"I'm. . .I'm sorry. I'm afraid it's been quite a day," she said ruefully. "Would you like to come in and tell me about this job?"

She stood back, and held the door open for him. He seemed to fill the small lounge room, and yet she doubted that he was any taller than Jack. As he sat down on the comfortable lounge chair, she eased herself onto the straight-backed kitchen chair she always sat in when visitors were present. She had found it far too embarrassing to have anyone she didn't know very well watch her undignified scramble to stand up from the lower, softer chair. When she looked up, he was watching her curiously.

Her chin rose. "What was the nature of the help you require?" she asked crisply.

He hesitated and she tensed, waiting for the inevitable question about her limp and stiff-legged gait. "Julie said you were a registered nurse and that you wanted a part-time position. She felt very concerned that you left so upset."

So much for her hasty exit before she had disgraced herself by revealing how disappointed she had been, thought Brenda grimly, but very relieved he hadn't asked the question she thought he might have.

"You've mentioned a Doctor Harrison and someone called Julie. Would Julie be the receptionist at Doctor Hickey's surgery?" She was tempted to add, "and the woman who kissed and hugged you so enthusiastically?"

He stared for a moment and then smiled slightly. "Didn't Julie tell you who she was? I'm afraid that sounds like her. She is Doctor Harrison, and also Doctor Hickey's daughter."

"Oh, she's a doctor!"

"Apparently the receptionist had to leave and she stayed on to see you, as they had been unable to reach you on the phone all day."

"I've been out since early this morning keeping appointments with Directors of Nursing and other people I hoped might have work I could do," she said, unable to prevent the bitterness that crept into her voice.

"Julie said you had excellent references and I think she was a little sorry her father's old temperamental receptionist had changed her mind at the last minute about retiring just yet," he said quickly and then paused. "Would you consider looking after a fifteen-year-old boy recovering from a back injury?" he asked abruptly. "I'm afraid, though, that there isn't any real nursing involved. At this stage, my brother needs someone mainly to keep an eye on him and try and keep him from doing anything stupid when I'm not home. Until I can get someone to do the housework, I would need you to help with that, also. Can you cook?" he shot at her.

"Yes, nothing fancy," Brenda said after a slight pause. Her mind was working quickly. "Would there be any lifting involved?"

"No, Rick is able to get out of bed and generally looks after himself, but he insists he can't do very much yet. He's recovering from spinal surgery, but has spent so much time flat on his back that he is bored silly and inclined to do too much once my back's turned."

He glanced at his watch uneasily. "In fact, I've been away too long today already. Until yesterday we had a housekeeper. She managed to fall and fracture her leg," he said grimly. "And Rick's mother chose this week, for some reason known only to herself, to go for a trip to the Goldcoast. I'm supposed to start work next week, which would mean Rick's being left by himself for most of the day. This morning I, too, have been busy. Appointments connected with my new job. I returned from the United States only a few days ago and can't afford to miss out on this opportunity. I just haven't got the time to go through the unemployment office to get someone suitable. We need you immediately."

Brenda felt bombarded by the spate of words, and a little

breathless. But a tiny feeling of excitement and hope began to rise. "How many hours a week would it involve?" she asked.

He suddenly looked uneasy. "I'm. . .hmm. . .afraid that's the catch. When I start work, it could involve my being called out at night. I know you only wanted part-time work and the hours you actually would be working could be very flexible, but I'm afraid I would need you to live in."

"Live in?" she asked.

The doubt in her voice made him spring to his feet and take a hasty stride across the room and back. He stopped beside her chair and looked intensely at her.

"Are you involved with anyone?" At the bewilderment that filled her eyes, he raked his hair back again and said quickly, "I know that Julie called you Miss, so I take it you aren't married. Is there anyone who would object to you living in the same house with me with only Rick as a chaperone?"

Sudden, unexpected pain stabbed Brenda's heart. No, she wasn't "involved" with anyone, nor married. That was one of the dreams that had vanished along with the career that she had found so challenging and satisfying. She lowered her head and stared at her tightly clenched hands. It would not be wise for her to go and live in this man's house. His attractiveness was far too potent. Instinct warned her against going but instinct would not provide a roof over her head! Besides, any man would quickly lose interest in her, she decided. She looked up at him and silently shook her head.

Blake looked even more uncomfortable. "What about that young man you kissed goodbye just before?"

"Doug? Doug's only seventeen!" Indignation loosened her tongue. "You were outside the flat then?"

"Well," the soft drawl hardened in his precise voice, "you

might say I was just very carefully pulling up after nearly being sideswiped by your friend's car."

Brenda bit her lip. "Oh, that."

"Yes, that!"

His eyes seemed to turn even darker when he looks annoyed, she noticed as she stared up at him.

To her surprise, he suddenly crouched down beside her chair. "You could ring Doctor Hickey and check me out if you like but, I can assure you, there won't be any funny business while you're working for me and living in my home." His voice was unexpectedly soft and earnest.

That deep well of mischief, which had been buried during those long months in a hospital bed, suddenly surfaced. "And when I'm not working for you and living in your house?" she murmured.

Something flared very briefly in his eyes, and she caught her breath. She had expected him to laugh again, and was startled and embarrassed when the dark eyes so close to her own suddenly turned very cool, and she had the feeling that in some deep part of him, he had withdrawn from her.

"You won't need to worry about that, either." His voice was crisp, the American accent suddenly not so pronounced. As spoke, he stood and moved back to the lounge chair. "Well, if you don't mind living in, would you be able to start immediately?" he added in a businesslike way.

He named a salary that made her blink and she heard herself agreeing that everything seemed satisfactory.

"How long will it take you to pack? We can have something to eat when we get there, and—"

Brenda sat up very straight. "You mean you want me to come with you now?" she gasped.

He frowned impatiently. "Haven't you been listening? I said it was urgent. We can't leave Rick alone any longer. It'll be dark soon and who knows what he's been up to."

"But you could go home now and pick me up tomorrow," she heard her voice begin to rise. "I've had a very exhausting day and there's no way I want to go out that door again tonight!"

"Tomorrow I have appointments all day and I simply can't spare the time. Besides, I don't want to leave Rick by himself two days in a row," he snapped. "You said you aren't involved with—"

"What's going on out there?" a new voice said sleepily.

"Jack!" Brenda's face lit up as she swung around. "When did you get home?"

The red-haired man who had just emerged from the bedroom, ran a large paw over his face, yawned mightily, and then grinned at her as she heaved herself out of her chair and swung as quickly as she could toward him. He gave her a huge kiss on the cheek and slipped his arm around her waist.

"Sometime before midday, I think. What time is it now? I was so close to home at daybreak I decided there was no place like my own bed, so I kept going. Thought I'd surprise you. But what did I find? The bird had flown!" The friendly grin he had aimed toward Blake slowly faded as he took in the astounded look of disapproval that was obvious on Blake's face as he eyed the bare chest and the loose pajama pants. "Who's your friend, Brennie?"

"Blake Warwyck. And I seem to have been wasting my time." His voice was tight with anger. "You don't really need a job, now, do you," he accused Brenda to her astonishment.

Brenda felt Jack's arm around her stiffen. She moved away from him and stared at Blake's dark angry face. A puzzled frown began to crease Jack's usually amiable features.

"Of course I need a job. This is Jack Browne. He's my—"

"Very good friend," Jack slipped in softly. He was now glaring suspiciously at Blake.

Brenda stared at the two men. What was the matter with the pair of them? Jack was certainly a very good friend, but much more than that. She looked up at him with a tinge of hurt. Before she could speak, Jack turned away and made for the large lounge chair.

"Sorry, but I guess I'll need more sleep to recover from the past couple of weeks," he muttered apologetically as he slouched down on the chair.

"I'd better be going then," said Blake curtly, and started for the door.

"But don't you want me to work for you anymore?" Brenda's voice sounded bewildered and hurt.

He paused. "Yes, I need you," he said reluctantly at last.

"Well then, aren't you going to wait until I throw a few things into a case?" Brenda heard herself say angrily.

Some undefinable look flashed into Blake's face. He looked at Jack hesitantly.

"Don't look at me, mate," shrugged Jack. "Brenda makes her own decisions. Where's the job?"

"At my home, looking after my young brother," said Blake briefly.

Jack yawned again. "Think you can handle it, love?"

Brenda was fed up with the pair of them. She stifled her own doubts. "I wouldn't go if I didn't think I could," she challenged him. He raised an eyebrow and, after a moment she added softly, "And if I thought it wasn't the right thing."

A loving smile touched Jack's face. "Good on yer, mate."

She smiled a little shakily back at him before starting for the bedroom.

"Just grab what you need for a couple of days. We can come back another time and get anything else you need," snapped Blake.

When she had disappeared, there was silence for a few moments in the room she had left.

"She's a good kid," Brenda heard Jack say softly at last.

After a moment of silence, she heard Blake move across the room and then the creak of a lounge chair as he sat down.

"If I didn't think so, I wouldn't be able to trust her with my young brother," Blake said just as softly. Then he added crisply and clearly, "I've read a couple of her excellent references."

Brenda felt an unexpected stab of disappointment at his businesslike tones.

"What's wrong with your brother?"

Brenda stopped gathering up some underwear to throw in a small case and waited for Blake's answer. She suddenly realized that she knew very little about the boy she was going to look after.

"Almost twelve months ago he injured his back in a car accident," Blake said slowly. "After the smash he had to spend a long time in a special spinal unit in a hospital in Sydney. Apparently he's been in and out of the hospital here in Newcastle since."

"Apparently?" Jack said enquiringly.

There was another brief silence and Brenda grabbed another culotte and a couple of her loose slacks.

"I've been overseas," said Blake. "Only just got back to Australia. They didn't tell me everything that's been happening."

And that hurt you somehow, thought Brenda, and then immediately wondered how she knew. She shrugged and then, instead of listening to the soft murmur of voices, she concentrated on trying to remember what she should take.

She grabbed her Bible first and then the daily devotional book Jack had given her. *I'm surely going to need these,* she thought a little grimly.

It wasn't a very big flat and she had to go through the lounge room to get to the bathroom to collect her toiletries. As she went past, she glanced at the two men. There was a chuckle from Jack at something the other man must have said.

She breathed a slight sigh of relief. Despite what Jack had said about her making her own decisions, she knew how protective of her he could be. He had been this way ever since his mother had held her by her hand and introduced her to Jack as his new little sister. She had seen the young teenage boy's face light up. To her absolute amazement he had given her a big hug and gently kissed her cheek. She had felt the tears prick her eyes at his enthusiastic, "Hi, Brennie!" and begun to wonder, and dare to hope again, that this time her foster family might become a real family. And so it had proved to be. Not only had she found a family of her own but they had introduced her to Jesus and a whole new life in a Christian home.

When she appeared a few minutes later with her small case, both men rose to their feet.

"I'll take that out to the car while you say goodbye," said Blake briskly and gave her a slight smile as he took it from her.

He held out his hand to Jack. Brenda was very relieved to feel the change in the atmosphere between the two men. Jack did not hesitate to shake hands with him.

"She'll be all right with me," Blake assured him. He hesitated, and then added as he looked steadily at Jack, "I'm a committed Christian, if that helps you to—"

Jack's eyes gleamed suddenly. "Great! It sure does." Then he stilled. "And yeah, I think she'll be fine with you. Just fine," his voice drawled softly.

Some unspoken communication seemed to pass between

them, and then they grinned at each other before Blake went toward the doorway.

"What was that all about?" Brenda asked curiously after he had disappeared.

"Never you mind," amusement sounded in Jack's voice. "You'd better not keep the man waiting. He's really worried about his kid brother." He gave her another big hug. "Goodbye, love. I hope you get on well. Don't let them expect too much of you. I thought we might have a chance to talk about the wedding. Make sure he knows he has to make other arrangements for that weekend, won't you? Cath and I sure can't get married without my little sister being there."

"Oh, Jack, I'm so very pleased you've found someone like Cathy. You're such a dear person and deserve the very best." Brenda's eyes felt damp as she clung to him for a moment.

"Well, I reckon I've sure got the best in my Cath. I need her strength in the Lord, too." Jack beamed proudly at her. "Now, off you go. Oh, you haven't got your crutches. I'll just go and—"

"No!" Brenda said sharply, and a little defiantly. "I'm not taking them with me."

He looked at her for a moment and then frowned. "Are you sure you're ready to leave them behind overnight?

She looked away from his searching glance. "I'll manage."

"Brennie, you did tell him you had an artificial leg, didn't you?" Jack asked sharply.

three

Brenda looked dumbly at Jack and shook her head.

Jack looked at her anxiously. "Oh, love, you should have told him. He could be expecting you to be able to do things you can't manage."

"I never deliberately. . .I mean. . .I didn't plan not to tell him," Brenda tried to defend herself. "It sort of. . .well. . . I collided with him in town today, and I felt like such an idiot!"

"Yes, he told me how you met."

"He did?"

"Didn't go into details. Just said you nearly fell when you met head-on," Jack said a little impatiently and then paused as another thought struck him. He looked at her intently and then his eyes began to twinkle. "He also said you were one of the most beautiful women who'd ever fallen into his arms."

"He did?" Brenda found herself beaming at him.

"Well, you are. Always have been," said Jack, matter-of-factly. "The natural way those streaks in your hair shine like old copper in the sunlight and the fact that your lovely face also reflects your inner beauty, has been drilled into me by many a smitten, would-be boyfriend. Some of the women I took out didn't like you much, though. Too much competition. I rarely went out with them again," he said reflectively.

"Jack!" For a moment Brenda didn't know if she was going to laugh or cry. Then any desire to smile left her.

"But how many have said that in the last few months? Mr. Warwyck didn't see much of me, did he?" The hurt she had never tried to hide from Jack was there in her voice.

"Brennie, please! You have to believe it doesn't really matter to people who know you. You're still very beautiful. How many times have we talked about the Scriptures putting far more emphasis on inner beauty? But besides that aspect, I know many, many women with a full count of ten toes who would give their eye teeth to be anywhere as near as attractive as you. You have to believe that, Bren."

"I really try, Jack dear. But since Robert broke off our engagement, I've realized that for a man. . .," she swallowed on the hard lump in her throat, "for men it's different."

She had never been able to put into words how ugly and repulsive she had felt, since the day she had suddenly opened her eyes from a deep sleep in her hospital bed, to find her fiancé staring down at her left leg. It had been only a couple of weeks since the accident. The ugly wounds on her right leg had still been heavily bandaged but the suture line on her left leg had needed drying out and had been left exposed. Because it had been hot, and she had not been expecting visitors so early in the day, she had thrown off all the covers.

Robert's normally well-tanned face had become pale; beads of sweat had stood out on his forehead. But it was the horror and loathing in his eyes that haunted her.

He had looked up and wordlessly stared at her. For one awful moment she had thought he had looked so sick that he might vomit. But he had turned and almost run from the room. She had still been so weak from the accident that the tears that began trickling down her face had turned into a torrent, which the worried hospital staff had tried in vain to stem. In the end, only the strong sedative they had been forced to give her had sent her into a restless sleep. She had never told Jack or Mum Browne. When Robert had broken off their engagement a few days later, they had been surprised that she had accepted it as calmly as she had.

Jack scowled. "That. . .that idiot! What a wimp of a man he turned out to be! And he called himself a Christian! He—"

The loud, long blast of a horn interrupted her thoughts. "I've got to go," said Brenda hurriedly, making for the door as fast as she could. By the time she reached the top of the steps, Blake Warwyck was standing at the bottom.

"I thought perhaps I'd better see whether you'd changed your mind," he said shortly and then turned away again as she started down.

By the time she reached the car, Blake was seated in the driver's seat with his seat belt already on. She didn't think much of the battered looking Holden, as she paused beside it. And she didn't think much of Mr. Warwyck's manners either, she decided. It was Jack who waited for her to settle before shutting the door for her. She was still putting on her own seat belt when the car was put into motion. There was only time for a quick wave to a frowning Jack and then they turned the corner and increased speed.

The inside of the station wagon was also very battered looking and certainly very dirty as well. She had a moment of doubt; perhaps she should have checked this stranger out. She knew she should have told him about her leg but she still didn't know just how she could broach the subject. She couldn't quite bring herself to say something like, "Oh, by the way, you haven't met Ermatroid yet, my fancy leg, you know!"

She glanced at him and studied the strong line of his jaw. He needed a shave. He was so dark that probably he needed to shave twice a day. That black hair badly needed a trim, too. The skin on his face and hands was much paler than someone with such smooth olive skin would normally have in January, unless he spent all his time indoors. But then, hadn't he said he'd been overseas? He would have come from their winter to this Australian summer. He really is very good looking, she decided for the umpteenth time. With a good tan, he would be devastating.

She looked away again, her hands clenched in her lap. *Who are you kidding?* she thought. He is devastating now. And what she really wanted was for him to continue to think she was beautiful, she admitted to herself.

"Have you ever been to Medowie?" he broke the silence to ask her.

Brenda found she had to clear her throat before she could answer. She felt him glance at her.

"Are you all right?" he asked her softly.

"People are always asking me if I'm all right," she flared suddenly.

There was silence. She bit her lip. That had sounded awful. "I'm sorry. I don't—"

"And you are always saying sorry," he interrupted quietly. There was the faintest hint of a smile in his voice. "I thought you might be interested in where you'll be living for the next few weeks."

"Oh, no! I should have asked you before and given the address to Jack. He'll be off again tomorrow."

"Well, I didn't really give you much time to think, did I?" All amusement had fled from his voice. "Don't fret. Your very good friend was not letting you go without a forwarding address. I gave it to him while you were packing."

"Thank you." Brenda felt like an idiot. What must he think of her? Not even demanding to know where he was taking her! "Jack's not just a good friend," she blurted out hurriedly. "He's my brother. . .my foster brother actually."

Blake turned his head sharply. Their eyes locked for a moment before he swung back to the road. She went hot. Why had she told him that? As she remembered what else Jack had said, she frowned. "I don't know why Jack told you he was only my friend."

"Don't you?" There was censorship in the deep tones. "I think I do," he added so softly that she wondered if she had heard correctly.

She glanced at him curiously, then she shrugged. What strange creatures men were sometimes, she silently pondered, and not for the first time over the years.

The car slowed down and stopped at another set of traffic lights. Brenda peered around her. She had not been taking any notice of the direction they had been traveling. Jack's flat was situated near the university and the Mater Hospital, several miles west of the city center of Newcastle. This was an intersection that came out onto the industrial highway to the north. It traveled east to west past the huge, sprawling Broken Hill Proprietary Steel Mill, as well as other heavy industries for which Newcastle was well known. It was a double-laned road that had been constructed to carry the large volume of traffic that flowed at each change of shift.

A number of smokestacks spewed out their varying shades of gray and white smoke. B.H.P. was the largest steel mill in Australia and mainly responsible in the past for the undeserved title of smog city, which outsiders had given this beautiful city only two hours' drive on the expressway north of Sydney. It had now spread, from the mouth of the wide Hunter River and the beautiful beaches and rolling surf of the Pacific Ocean, mainly toward the south and west.

As the car joined the traffic on the wide, still-busy thoroughfare, Brenda asked slowly, "Did you say, Medowie?"

"Yes. Know it?"

"But isn't that way north, past Williamstown Air Force Base, near the Grahamstown Dam?" When he nodded, she said with rising concern, "But that's a long way from Newcastle. I took it for granted we'd be in the city."

"It's only about a forty-minute drive usually. Oh, no!"

It wasn't until the car swung sharply to the side of the road, that Brenda heard the soft thumping that heralded a flat tire. After the car stopped, Blake put his head down on the hands still clenched on the steering wheel and groaned.

"That's all I need! I hope you've kept the spare in good condition, Betsy! Stay there," he barked as Brenda opened her door the same time as he did.

Brenda looked around the dirty, rather dilapidated interior of the old station wagon and hoped that this Betsy, whoever she was, had kept the spare better than the rest of the car. By the howl of rage that issued from the back of the car a few minutes later, she knew that Betsy hadn't!

"As flat as a pancake! Women!" she heard him roar.

She scrambled from the car and joined him. The spare tire was leaning against the car and Blake's hair looked as though two hands had been pushed through it! Her lips twitched. "The nearest service station is at Mayfield," she said carefully.

"I know the service stations are at Mayfield," he roared. "But there's no way I'm rolling this. . .this thing several kilometers to Mayfield!"

He looked helplessly at the large, empty paddock

stretching back to some industrial buildings. Across the highway, the houses all faced another street, with only their back yard fences in view.

"I suppose there's a phone over there somewhere," he muttered savagely.

Brenda spotted a familiar vehicle waiting at the traffic lights they had just left. She stepped farther out onto the road and started to wave both arms energetically at it.

"What are you doing now? Trying to get yourself run over?"

A pair of hands grabbed her around the waist and nearly threw her off balance as he hauled her back. A truck roared past with a derisive blast of its horn. The strong hands pulled her back into his body as a taxi screeched to a halt behind them.

For a breathless moment she allowed her body to lean into him and then she turned her head toward him and said demurely, "Your taxi, sir."

She felt his grip on her waist tighten for a moment and then his lips brushed against her cheek before he released her and turned toward the taxi driver striding toward them.

"Not just a pretty face," she thought she heard him say before greeting the other man.

Her body felt an unusual warmth where his had touched hers and her cheek felt as though a flame had flickered across it. That annoyed her. She scrubbed at it with one hand.

After a brief conversation, the men started back to the taxi with the tire. Brenda returned to the Holden for her handbag before following them. As she opened the back door of the cab, Blake called out to her. "Why don't you wait in the car. I shouldn't be too long."

She ignored him, sat on the seat of the taxi, lifted her

legs in, and slammed the door—hard! Blake's head appeared at the window, one eyebrow raised.

"You dragged me away before I even had time to swallow one mouthful of the coffee I had just made. I haven't had a bite to eat since well before lunch. I am not going to swelter in that car. And I am going to have at least a cold drink at the service station before you drag me all the way out to. . .to Medowie." Her voice was very controlled as she glared at him.

He glared back for a moment and then the expression on his face changed and he disappeared. He had suddenly looked very concerned, she thought with a feeling of satisfaction.

The taxi driver entered the car. "Hello," he said cheerfully. "Just as well you waved when you did, I was just starting to answer a call on the two-way radio."

A few moments later Blake joined him in the front seat and then they were off. When they reached the service station, Blake asked the taxi driver to wait for a few minutes after getting the tire out of the boot.*

His curt "stay there" to Brenda were the first words to her since he had joined the driver in the front seat of the cab. The two men had talked quietly together and being ignored had increased the anger brewing in her. It had been a foul day and this rude man was foul, too.

When Blake strolled back, for some reason she thought he looked rather pleased with himself. "Would you take us farther down Maitland Road, please?" he asked the driver pleasantly.

Brenda shut her eyes. She was hungry and thirsty and didn't know where they were going now. The cab stopped.

"I am not setting one foot out of this vehicle until I know where we are and what we're doing," she said so loudly

*Trunk of a car

that two male heads swung toward her in unison.

"Are you all right?" asked the concerned voice of the driver.

She closed her eyes again and gritted her teeth. There was a stifled sound from Blake, which sounded suspiciously like a smothered laugh.

"Yes, she's fine, thanks," she heard Blake reply.

Then her door was pulled open and a pair of twinkling eyes were shining at her. She blinked and felt the anger begin to drain away. Twice in one day, she had let anger get a grip on her!

Without a word, he reached across and released her seat belt. His hand brushed against her hip and she gave an involuntary shiver. *What is the matter with me?* she thought furiously. He stood back and waited for her to get out. Suddenly she felt too weary to fight him and accepted his steadying hand as she stood up.

"I'm the one who's very sorry this time," he said softly as he slipped an arm around her waist and turned her toward the building near them. It was a Chinese restaurant.

"I don't know why I didn't ask if I could ring Rick from your place. They let me use the phone at the service station. His friend from next door answered and said everything was fine and that they were just having their tea. So I thought it was about time we ate, too. I arranged for the new tire to be put on for us and for the spare to be replaced also. I'm not game to travel again without it," he finished grimly. "I could wring Betsy's neck." He reached out to push open the restaurant door for her. "Hope you like Chinese food."

"I love it," she sighed gratefully.

"Well, perhaps you'd better tell me more about my job," Brenda said after they had ordered their meal and sat sipping icy cold mineral water drinks. "Who's Betsy? Or perhaps you had better start with your mother. How come she left on a trip so soon after your arrival back in the country?"

Blake put down his glass slowly and stared at her. "My, my. You don't hesitate to ask personal questions, do you?"

"Oh, I'm sor—" she stopped abruptly. Then she tilted her chin at him. "No, I'm not. There are things I'll need to know in order to be able to help your brother and knowing why your mother has gone away when he's recovering from surgery is surely one of them."

He sighed. "You're right of course. But the simple answer is, I don't know. She's been under a lot of strain the past two months, and did seem very tired and full of nerves, but it would have been best if I could have spent a bit more time with her before she went. And you're wrong about her being my mother. My mother died when I was twelve years old."

"But you said your brother's mother. Oops, that makes him your halfbrother."

"Brilliant!" he smiled gently at her confusion. "Dad remarried when I was fourteen. And to answer your next question, my father died two months ago." A deep sadness filled his eyes until they seemed almost black in the soft light.

Brenda impulsively reached over and touched the back of his hand resting on the white tablecloth. He turned it over and clung to hers. It seemed perfectly natural to leave it nestled there.

"And you were a long way away," she murmured understandingly.

The grip on her hand tightened convulsively. "It was very bad. I was working near New York and had to break my contract, so it's taken me all this time to get back. Originally I'd intended to stay for another six months. There were no vacant seats on a plane to get me home in time for the funeral." His other hand began to restlessly trace patterns on the cloth.

He was so deep in unpleasant memories that except for that grip on her hand, Brenda would have been excused for thinking that he had forgotten she was there. She remained silent and suddenly found herself praying for the right words.

After taking a deep breath, he spoke so softly she had to strain to hear. "She told me he knew about his heart condition before I went overseas. He never told me."

There was deep hurt here, Brenda thought. *Somehow he had felt betrayed, even unloved?* And then she wondered how she was so sure she was right.

The first course arrived and, with a start, he released her hand. It tingled and Brenda put it in on her lap and tried to unobtrusively stretch her fingers to help the circulation. She looked up to find him studying her with a wondering, slightly puzzled expression.

When the waiter had gone, Blake offered her the bowl of fried rice to go with her Mongolian lamb. After he had also helped himself, he looked across the table before starting to eat and drawled slowly, "Now, I think you should tell me a bit about your background."

four

The food Brenda had just put in her mouth suddenly tasted like sawdust. She swallowed it slowly and then reached for another mouthful of drink.

"I'm like you, Blake," she said harshly, and not very truthfully. "No parents." She refused to think of the dirty, drunken wreck of a woman she had been taken from so long ago and had never heard from since. She forced a smile. "Although I do have a foster mother who's a real darling. But what about Rick? What's been wrong with his back?"

He hesitated for a moment as he stared at her intently and then, to her immense relief, accepted the change of topic.

"Car accident. Less than twelve months ago. That's another thing I wasn't told much about. I had no idea of the full story until his mother filled me in the night I got home. I was suffering from jet lag and I'm still not sure if I understand all of it."

She looked at him a little curiously. She didn't like the way he referred to his stepmother as "his mother," and did not, at the very least, use her name.

He went on to tell her that apparently Rick had been trying to hitch a ride home from Newcastle when some crazy woman had started trying to take him to Sydney. The car had skidded. She had lost control and plowed into a tree.

Brenda shuddered. "The same thing happened to me. It's

the most dreadful few seconds, when you know you're going to crash, and there's not a thing you can do," she said thoughtlessly.

"Is that when you injured your legs?" he asked softly.

She had been about to put her glass down. Her arm jerked and somehow the glass flew out of her hand, a stream of fluid shooting across the table. Blake started mopping it up with his napkin and the waiter rushed over to help. By the time the waiter had insisted on placing a large clean napkin over the damp tablecloth, removed their empty plates, and brought her another drink of mineral water, Brenda had recovered.

She was thankful when Blake did not persist with his question and instead said, "Rick spent a few months in a spinal unit in a Sydney hospital and has been having treatment ever since. They've apparently been almost as worried about his emotional and mental problems. Or so his mother told me," he added a little skeptically. "He did have a concussion initially, but his general behavior to her, and especially to Betsy, has been appalling. . .once again, according to his mother. He's nothing like the happy boy I said goodbye to." Concern deepened his voice. "He certainly seems very withdrawn and bitter. Perhaps you can find some way of finding out what's eating into him."

"Well, I've never had much to do with teenagers," Brenda said doubtfully. "Doug's been the only one I've ever spent much time with and he's a good bit older than your halfbrother. But I'm certainly willing to try."

"Great!" He gave a sigh and relaxed. "Now, let's find out more about you. What music do you like the most?"

She tensed, ready to ward off unwelcome questions. "Before we get onto me," she said hurriedly, "you told Jack you were a Christian. Is. . .is your brother. . .does he have a personal relationship with God?" she ended up hesitantly as his face darkened again.

"No," he answered abruptly. "My mother, when she was alive, always took me to church and Sunday school but my. . .my father only scoffed at all that useless 'religious stuff' as he called it. And my stepmother's even worse. University didn't help me one bit, either. It's only been the last few months, while I was in America, that I've come to grips with spiritual issues and Christ's claims on my life. I. . .I know there's an awful lot of things to be sorted out in my life still. And what about you?" he asked abruptly and with an oddly challenging look.

"Well, I. . .I. . .I've been a Christian since my teens," Brenda found herself saying hesitantly, wondering if one day she might be able to talk to this man about some of the doubts and questions that had at times filled her mind since the accident. She had been afraid of upsetting Jack and his mother by pouring them out to them. They'd had enough to cope with at the time.

"You asked me what kind of music I liked," she hastened to add brightly and ignored the curious glint in his eyes as she began to babble about her love for country and western music.

To her relief, he followed her lead and, with a feeling of relief, she found herself relaxing. During the rest of their meal, she found herself enjoying sharing their likes and dislikes in sports as well as music.

It turned out they were both ardent supporters of the Australian cricket team. Brenda listened enviously as he told her about a day he had spent at Lord's famous grounds in England, watching one of the fights for the Ashes, which she had only caught glimpses of on a hospital television. He had always enjoyed soccer rather than rugby, whereas she followed the Sydney rugby league competition fervently. They argued over the different football codes until Blake suddenly glanced at his watch.

"Oh, no. We've been here too long. I'm glad that service station is open twenty-four hours!"

He bustled her away, refusing point-blank when she offered to pay her share of the bill. It took them quite a while to find another taxi to take them back for the tire and on to the Holden station wagon. As they headed off again, it was close to nine o'clock and there was nowhere near the volume of traffic as there was earlier. It wasn't far before they turned north onto the Nelson Bay Road and were soon on the bridge over the wide Hunter River. The road then swung back east for a while, following the river. The lights of the steel mill coming down to the river's edge on the other side were reflected in the water and she could also see the lights of a large ship at anchor.

There was a comfortable silence between them. Brenda was encased in a quiet glow of happiness. She had thoroughly enjoyed their conversation and was glad she had discovered they had so much in common when it came to music and sports. Robert had been a resident doctor and their times together had more often than not been spent talking about work. He wasn't at all interested in sports and he'd liked heavy metal music, which she couldn't stand. One thing that had often troubled her had been his reluctance to talk about spiritual matters.

Brenda decided that she liked this man very much. But that's where this has to stop, she told herself firmly. She must remember he was only her employer and be thankful that he would be pleasant to work for.

After they had gone over the Stockton Bridge and were heading north again, she remembered something. She gave a little chuckle and turned to him impulsively. "You never did tell me who the wicked Betsy is. Is that your stepmother's name?"

"I'll have you know my stepmother's name is Annette . . .never shortened to Ann, please note," his deep voice was wry, "Dear Betsy I only met when I arrived home. Apparently Annette employed her as a live-in housekeeper just before Dad died. I think Annette wanted to be free to do some study or something. She was rather vague about it all. As I said, we really didn't have time for much of a chat."

His voice sounded rather grim again and Brenda, trying to see his face in the dark, regretted asking him about it.

"There's something about Betsy. . .," he hesitated and she saw him shrug his shoulders before continuing, "I suppose I'm just angry with the poor woman because the timing of her landing in the hospital was so bad. And live-in housekeepers in this part of the world are very difficult to find, Annette assured me before she left. She warned me to treat her with kid gloves, so Betsy would still be there when Annette gets home. Annette took her own car, or more accurately Dad's car, with her. This is the one Betsy has been using."

They lapsed into silence again and Brenda's thoughts turned to Blake's meeting with Jack. What had gotten into the pair of them? The air had almost bristled between them at first. She thought of the enthusiastic greeting she had given Jack. Perhaps Blake didn't like displays of affection in front of him. But he had enjoyed his display in front of her with that blond doctor, she decided.

Jack owned a couple of semitrailers and was often away for long stretches at a time, hauling freight interstate. She had been so glad to see him. It had been the first time she had lived by herself since the accident and she had been lonely at times. He had persuaded her to use his flat while she was trying to get work in Newcastle.

After her final discharge from the rehabilitation center, she had been living with Mum Browne in Sydney. But she disliked the thought of working there, and had wanted to return to Newcastle where she had obtained her nursing diploma at the university and where most of her friends lived. She had been there only a few days when she had developed a sore spot on her leg where her prosthesis had rubbed when she had spent too much time, too soon on Ermatroid in the heat. So she had been confined again within four walls, forced to use the crutches again until the sore spot disappeared and she could wear the leg again.

She hoped today's marathon had not caused any more problems. She bit her lip as she stared blindly through the windscreen.* Perhaps she had been foolish leaving those hated crutches behind.

"You said Jack was your foster brother. He said he's known you since you were a kid." The soft, deep tones startled her.

"He sure has." She gave a soft, reminiscent laugh. "I was only ten when I went to live with them. Had just met his mother, and found out she had a fourteen-year-old son. I had learned to hate teenage boys and was dreading meeting him. Then this freckle-faced kid, with his red hair standing on end, gave me a big hug, and actually kissed me on the cheek. I've loved him ever since."

Blake was silent. Brenda thought back to that time when she had been so terrified of once again having to live with another bunch of strangers. For about two years she had moved from government institutions to numerous foster homes. But no one had really wanted the scared, sullen

*Windshield of a car

little girl who had been so uncooperative and caused nothing but trouble.

"You said your foster mother was a darling. That's Jack's mother?" There was a hint of constraint in the suddenly husky voice.

"Yes. Mum's cared for me, prayed endlessly for me, smacked me when I needed it, but has always been there when I needed her."

"I'd like to meet her someday. She sounds like quite a woman. What about Jack's father?"

"He was wonderful, too. He died last year. Only their faith in Christ and their church family's support got them through that." Her voice was sad. "Dad died just before—" she stopped abruptly.

"Before your accident?"

"Yes," she said curtly, and was relieved when he merely said, "You've had a rough year," and then added quietly, "well, this is it." The car slowed down before turning into a long driveway. "Hmmm. Looks as though Rick's gone to bed."

As the car stopped, Brenda peered through the windscreen at a large, single-storied house. The only light she could see was the one over the front entrance. And what an entrance!

"It's huge!" she gasped.

"Yes. Dad had this built on five acres, just before Mum died. He rented it out, and we lived in Newcastle until he married Annette." The voice was expressionless. "You go ahead, and I'll put this in the garage straight away, and bring your bag."

When he joined her, he put a key in the door and then hesitated. He put her bag down decisively. "If I don't do this now, it will be my last chance for a long time. Especially if. . .," he murmured as he turned toward her.

As he reached out and ran a light finger over her lips, she stared at him uncomprehendingly. A jolt of electricity shot through her and then the soft expression on his face mesmerized her. She stood rigidly as he took a step toward her and held her by the shoulders. She had barely met the man. Surely he wasn't going to. . .to—

Warm, tentative lips tasted hers. When she didn't stir, he sighed deeply and took a step forward. Warm, strong arms slipped around her. Then those lips were touching hers again, very tenderly at first, and then her lips seemed to become one with his, and the world shook around her. She wondered for a moment if another earthquake had struck, but then his lips trailed down her neck. A wave of flame swept through her from top to toe.

"Blake! You—"

His mouth returned, and it seemed as though he took her very breath into himself. Her lips and body seemed to have a mind of their own. She clung to him.

It was Blake who at last lifted his head. "You're so very beautiful," he murmured. Then he slowly moved his hand and lifted it to tuck a strand of hair gently behind her ear. Then he sighed deeply again as he released her and stepped back.

She felt incredibly deprived of his warmth, her flesh still tingling, alive, longing for his touch.

His gaze wandered over her flushed face. "I think perhaps I should fire you here and now, Brenda Sparks," he said at last in a very unsteady voice.

She gasped. Her trembling hands went up to her still tingling lips. "What. . .what did you do that for?" she managed to gasp at last.

"Because I've wanted to ever since you clung to me in

that corridor." White teeth gleamed in a slightly crooked smile. "And once you enter that door, you're under my roof, in my employ, and I did promise no funny business."

That was funny business? It had been very serious for her!

She stared at him. He moved toward her again and then paused. He sighed regretfully and turned to open the door. Her feet felt rooted to the spot.

"If you don't come in now, I'll be happy to oblige again," he said.

Still in a daze, she moved toward him but, once inside, she caught her breath. He had switched on the indoor light and a small chandelier lit up the large foyer. The interior did more than justice to the imposing entrance. In one corner there was a veritable forest of ferns and creepers. A landscape painting of a sunburned Australian countryside adorned another wall, and Brenda guessed correctly that it was an original. The house was beautifully cooled by ducted air conditioning, she noticed.

"This way." Blake was staring at her intently. He sounded a little impatient, so she followed him through a spacious lounge room and into a wide corridor. They passed a couple of closed doors before he paused at last. He flung a door open and waited for her to enter first.

Here, too, no expense had been spared. She thought for one brief, slightly hysterical moment, that she had entered a room she had once seen in a magazine. It was beautifully furnished with a light maple, solid timber bed and matching dressing table. The pale cream curtains and bedspread Brenda recognized at once. She had once drooled over them in a large department store and reluctantly decided that a nurse's salary could not possibly afford it.

"It's very beautiful," she said reverently.

He flung her case on the bed and strode back to the doorway. "I may be gone in the morning when you get up. Take it easy on your first day. Rick can show you around." With those abrupt words, he disappeared.

She stared blankly after him. He hadn't even shown her the bathroom, not even said good night. But he had more than adequately said good night outside! Never before had she responded to a kiss like that. Not even with Robert! What had gotten into her? She shook her head. She must be more tired than she thought.

She moved abruptly over to the bed and unlocked her case. She took out the few things she had crammed in and then looked around to see where to hang her clothes. Looking around the large room, she saw another door. When she opened it, she gasped again. There was a huge walk-in wardrobe and her very own bathroom! How large was this house?

When trying to relax at last in her very comfortable bed, she found she could not go to sleep. As she tossed and turned, she irritably wished he had at least shown her where the kitchen was. She wouldn't have minded a hot drink before going to bed. Why had he packed her off to bed and left so abruptly?

After that kiss, perhaps he didn't trust her not to grab him again, she decided grimly. The conceit of the man! Who did he think he was, kissing her like that? She ignored the little voice that reminded her she had kissed him back. She rolled over on her stomach and buried her face in the pillow, trying to dislodge the memory of the way her body had responded to him.

At last she fell asleep, but when she eventually stirred, it was to the realization that her sleep had been restless and disturbed by dreams she could not properly remember.

The sound of a car brought her wide awake. She looked at the dainty little clock on the dressing table. Seven o'clock! She yawned and stretched. Time to get up and meet his brother—oops, stepbrother, she corrected herself.

With some difficulty she had a quick shower, glad of a plastic stool she managed to manuever into the recess. Then, wincing as she pulled on the thick woolen sock over a couple of tender, red spots on the stump, she at last quickly eased on her leg, pressing the Velcro-covered straps carefully in place. She dressed as quickly as she could in loose fitting slacks and a tee shirt, before hesitantly making her way back toward the front entrance. She was very tempted to open a few of the closed doors she passed, but resisted. It would be just her luck to be caught by this Rick.

In the large lounge room, she looked around. *My, my!* This was luxurious! *I bet that is a genuine leather lounge,* she thought with awe. In the foyer, she hesitated for a moment, and then walked through one of the doors that led off of it and found herself in a dining room equally as large as the lounge room. A highly polished cedar table was surrounded by plush, dark red, velvet-covered chairs. Sparkling crystal gleamed from behind the glass doors of a cedar cabinet. The same luxurious cream carpet as in the lounge room spread across the floor to two large bay windows.

She heard a faint sound from a door that led off of it. Taking a deep breath, she moved forward and entered a surprisingly homey kitchen.

A dark-haired boy was sitting at a table. He was putting a spoonful of breakfast cereal into his mouth as she appeared in the doorway.

"Good morning, you must be—" she started to say cheerfully, but broke off as he raised his head slowly and looked at her miserably.

Everything blurred for a moment, and she shook her head in a vàin attempt to clear it. She must be mistaken. He looked just like—

"Hello, Miss Sparks," he said unsteadily, and then burst out, "why did you have to come here!"

"Percy?" she whispered in a daze. Then her voice rose even as she began to feel very weak in the legs. "But it can't be!" she exclaimed. "You're dead. They. . .they told me you were dead!"

five

The boy stood up slowly and stiffly. He was thin and gangly, his hair was very dark, but not as black as Blake's.

"It *is* Percy!"

She swung toward him and gripped the back of a chair as a wave of faintness swept over her again.

"Someone told me. . .I asked. . .they said you. . .you'd gone. I always thought that meant you were dead! Oh, thank God, thank God! Oh, I'm so pleased. . .relieved you aren't. . ."

A startled expression chased away some of the hostility she had seen in his face as he glared at her. Her dazed eyes swept around the room swiftly, before focusing on him again.

"What. . .what are you doing here?" she asked faintly.

"I live here."

"Here? Are you staying with Mr. Warwyck?"

He stared blankly at her for a moment and then gave one quick jerk of the head in acknowledgment.

She moved shakily around the chair, and almost fell onto it. "What. . .what happened to you?"

He continued to stare at her silently.

She took a deep breath. "I mean, were you badly injured?"

"I. . .I. . .my back was hurt," he said slowly and reluctantly. "I was unconscious for some time. Apparently they. . .they put me in a helicopter." He swallowed convulsively. "I asked about you. They said you had only broken your legs."

She closed her eyes. Her initial feeling had been one of overwhelming gladness that she had not, after all, been responsible for this boy's death. Now she remembered his actions leading up to the accident.

She opened her eyes and stared at him scornfully. "Did you really care, Percy?"

He looked away. "Of course I cared." His voice was little more than a whisper. "I. . .I've had nightmares ever since," he burst out. "Why did you come here? Does Blake know?"

For a moment she felt bewildered. "Blake? What's he got to do with our accident?"

She saw him tense, but he bit his lip and just stared at her. The faint cleft in his chin caught her eye. The way his hair came to a peak in the middle—no wonder she had thought Blake looked familiar! Then she suddenly remembered what Blake had said about his brother.

"It was all lies, wasn't it?" she said slowly, but her mind was racing, remembering. "You told us your name was Percival, Percival Barwick. Only you liked to be called Percy, and Barwick was spelled with an 'i.' Only that wasn't your real name, was it? It must be Rick, and Warwyck, spelled with a 'y.' "

His face went very pale. "You wouldn't stop pestering me," he burst out defensively. "First that other lady at the service station, and then when you arrived—"

"Yes, we were very foolish trying to find out a scared kid's name and where he came from so we could take him home before he ruined his life, weren't we?" Brenda said sarcastically. "And I've had nightmares, too!"

She paused, forced now to remember the agony of that time, and the guilt. The guilt of never being able to see his parents and having a chance to explain, to tell them how sorry she was that their son was dead. "You see, I tried to find your family when I got out of hospital," she said softly and bitterly. "It was no wonder I couldn't find them, was it Rick?"

She felt like screaming out her anguish and pain at him. He walked awkwardly toward her. His eyes were burning in his dead-white face.

"I wish I had died." His voice sounded old and defeated. "I haven't been really free of pain since then and am so . . .so useless I can't even. . . And I know this last operation on my spine was supposed to stop that. Everyone keeps telling me to have patience. But even if the pain stops, I won't be able to play many sports or do any heavy lifting." He stared down at her bitterly and then turned to walk out of the room.

"Where do you think you're going?" she asked sharply.

He didn't stop. "I'm not supposed to stand very long. I still have to lie flat most of the day."

She let him go then. She needed time to come to grips with the fact that Blake's brother was Percy, the boy who had haunted her ever since the accident. She gave a small sob as the memories she had tried to stifle came thick and fast.

The car had slammed into the trees and his body had been flung across her. The feel of its limp weight had often been part of her nightmares. She had called out to him and then managed to push his head back. From somewhere in his hair, blood had been trickling down over his face.

She had cried out desperately to God, "Oh, don't let him die. Please, don't let him die."

And then she had wondered where God was and why He had apparently deserted her. Then there had been blood, so much blood. Something had been pressing on her own legs. She had tried to move them. Agony had gripped her. Someone had started screaming before the welcome blackness had fallen over her like a blanket.

When she had come back to a world of pain and flashing lights, the boy's body had been gone. There were peoples' voices near her. She still had the weight on her legs, and had tried to call out, but no one answered her before she lapsed again into unconsciousness. As they had lifted her battered body onto a stretcher, she had come to again and managed to ask the harried rescue worker where Percy was. The first few days that followed in the hospital were only a blurred memory.

She shuddered. Many times since then she'd questioned God, in the darkness and pain of the night, about that poor stranger's death. No one had mentioned the boy to her, not even Mum during all those long hours she had given Brenda the unfailing love, support, and spiritual help she had so desperately needed. There had been some internal damage as well as the battered legs, so it had been several weeks before she had been mobile enough to try and find out where the boy had lived and then to discover that the Newcastle address he had given them had been a false one.

And here he was, Blake's brother. The boy Blake was so worried about.

Tears started trickling down her face. At first she wasn't sure if they were tears caused by the flood of dreadful memories or tears of thankfulness that the boy was still alive or tears of rising anger and bewilderment. She remembered what Blake had told her about his brother's accident. Something about some dreadful woman taking him to Sydney. Anger started to gain the upper hand and, with an impatient hand, she brushed away the moisture on her face.

She stormed through the dining room and started toward the bedrooms. "Perc—Rick, where are you?"

She stopped for a moment to listen. There was not a sound to indicate where he might be.

"Rick!" she bellowed. "Answer me this minute!"

She flung open the first door on the right. The large, king-sized bed and the luxurious furnishings told her this must be the master bedroom, Annette's room. She retreated quickly. She heard a faint sound, and swung around. A slight, wide-eyed girl, about Rick's age, stood behind her.

"Who are you?" Brenda snapped.

"M. . .Melinda. Melinda Wood." The blond, jean-clad figure took a hesitant step forward and then a more determined one. "Who are you?" she asked politely.

"Brenda Sparks. What are you doing here?"

"I've come to milk the goats."

"Goats?" said Brenda weakly. A rising tide of hysteria made her want to laugh and scream at the same time. "What goats?"

"Mrs. Warwyck's. Were you trying to find Rick?"

Brenda took a deep breath. "Yes," she said abruptly.

"He's usually lying down on the veranda." The girl hesitated, then said very firmly, "You sounded mad with him. I don't know who you are, but you are not to upset him." She looked Brenda over assessingly. As Brenda was still trying to make up her mind whether to laugh or cry, the girl continued scornfully. "I suppose you're one of Blake's old girlfriends. Well, let me tell you, he won't like it if you upset his brother. Rick's been very down since his father died and he doesn't need someone like you yelling at him."

Before she could say a word, Melinda Wood brushed past her, hurried down the long corridor, and went past wide open glass doors at the end of it.

Brenda's anger faded and her sense of humor began to surface. This boy had lost his father recently, after all. Lucky for Rick to have such a champion! She heard a murmur of voices and slowly moved toward them. Then she paused briefly and leaned against the wall. A voiceless prayer for strength and wisdom whelmed through her being.

At long last she moved forward. The corridor opened onto a bright, cheerful room that took up the full width of that part of the house. Comfortable cane furniture was positioned in front of a large television in one corner. A couple of tables, obviously used for many and varied activities by the paraphernalia scattered over them, were also in the room.

A phone started to shrill. Brenda hesitated for a moment, and then spotted it next to a computer set up in another corner of the room. She let it ring another couple of times and, when Rick did not appear, she hurried over and picked up the receiver.

"Hello, Brenda Sparks speaking," she said briskly.

There was a brief pause. "That sounds just like a nursing sister." Blake's drawl held a trace of amusement.

Brenda felt a faint tingle. She swallowed rapidly and managed to say very calmly, "I guess that's because I have been one for some time, Mr. Warwyck."

Another short silence. Then, "My name is still Blake." His voice had stiffened. "My early appointment has been postponed and I wanted to make sure you were all right. I hope you slept well?"

"I took a little while to get to sleep." Brenda closed her eyes. Why had she said that? Now he might think his kiss had kept her awake. She continued hurriedly, and not quite truthfully, "I suppose it was the strange bed." To her annoyance, her voice sounded a little breathless.

"I didn't sleep either." His voice had deepened. "I realized this morning that I didn't offer you a drink, or even show you the common courtesy any guest should expect, such as showing you where the kitchen and facilities were." He paused. His voice sounded very husky as he murmured, "I thought it safer to get out of your room fast."

Brenda gasped at the undertones. "Mr. Warwyck, you said. . .you said—"

His sigh cut her off. "I know, no funny business." He was silent again.

A voice sounded in the background like an amplified message. It had seemed all along, from the background noises, as though he were on a public phone somewhere, but Brenda caught a couple of words, and thought it sounded very familiar. Why would he be ringing from the hospital?

"I've got to go," he said hurriedly. "Is Rick all right?"

Brenda sought for something to say. She couldn't very well say, "Well, I've just discovered he's not dead as I've thought for nearly twelve months!" or, "I was just about to track down your dear brother, and perhaps give him a piece of my mind!"

"Brenda?" Her name was snapped out. Her hesitation had made him more tense and worried.

She called on her professional training of perfecting non-committal answers when necessary and said as briskly as she could, "I think we may have a few things to sort out, but I'll cope."

"Good. If he's too obnoxious, tell him he'll have me to deal with." The voice boomed again in the background. "Look, I've got to go. I'm not sure just when I'll be home but be assured it will be as soon as possible." He sounded harassed, and then the phone clicked as he hung up.

For a moment, she stared at the phone receiver in her hand and then slowly replaced it. Wherever he was, someone wanted a Doctor Somebody-or-other. Strange, she thought, that last night he never once mentioned what work he actually did.

A pair of large sliding doors at one end of the room looked as though they might lead onto a veranda. She heard the faint murmur of voices again. As her hand touched the door, she heard Rick's voice rise loudly. The despair and fear in it caught her by the throat.

"Oh, Lindy, why did Dad have to die? Why did Mum make all those arrangements to go away in such a hurry the minute she knew Blake was arriving? I'm not sorry Betsy's not here anymore, but why did he have to bring this woman here? He said it was to keep me company." The depth of bitterness that accompanied the short laugh and the insinuation in the tone of voice shocked Brenda.

"Why do you think he brought me here then, Rick?" Brenda asked.

At the sound of her stern voice, two pairs of eyes swung around. Brenda noted that Rick pulled his hand away from Melinda's clasp. Two spots of color appeared on his pale cheekbones.

He stared defiantly at her for a moment, before his eyes dropped from her direct glare, and he turned his head away. He was lying on a full-sized bed with only one pillow under his head. The bed was pushed up against the wall of a wide veranda that was fully screened. A couple of outdoor lounges and a fancy wrought-iron table with matching chairs were scattered around the area.

"Rick?" Brenda's voice demanded an answer.

"Oh, leave him alone!" Melinda burst out.

"But I can't do that, Melinda," she replied in a milder voice. "You see, Mr. Warwyck did bring me here to keep Rick company, but I understand he also needs someone to generally look after the cooking and house until Betsy is on her feet again."

"I offered to help and Mum said she would do what she could," said Melinda.

"But don't the school holidays finish in another couple of weeks? And from what Mr. Warwyck said, I don't think the housekeeper will be out of hospital that soon."

"Ann will be home by then. We don't need strangers here!" Rick said.

Rick's voice was full of bravado but, as Brenda studied his face, she caught a glimpse of unmistakable fear and uncertainty. Was it to do with his mother's return or was he trying to make sure she allowed Melinda to think they were indeed strangers?

"You mean your mother?" Brenda asked.

"Of course he does," said Melinda rudely.

Brenda looked at her steadily and the girl had the grace to blush and look away.

"Your brother said you would be able to show me around the house this morning," Brenda said.

Rick stared back at her, his lips tightly pressed together.

Deciding the best attitude to take might be to ignore the hostility of the two youngsters, she moved over to the edge of the veranda and looked out. The house was built in the shape of a U and the two wings were separated by a beautifully landscaped garden. As she looked away to the right, she could see that no expense had been spared on the spacious yard, either. Past a large barbecue area, smooth-barked, old gum trees towered into the sky, casting welcome shade on large portions of neatly kept lawn and brightly flowering shrubs.

"You have a very beautiful home. Where do you keep the goats?" As the silence that greeted her remark lengthened, Brenda wondered what was happening behind her. Keeping her back determinedly to them, she opened a sliding screen door. Closing it firmly behind her and, very thankful to see a rail to lean on, she began to carefully descend down the short flight of cement steps.

Huge staghorns were clinging to the trunks of a couple of the trees and, in the center, she saw a high fence behind a bank of many different-colored hibiscus. The lawn was beautifully kept. They must use a lot of water to keep it so green at this time of the year, she mused.

The screen door squeaked open and closed, and Melinda joined Brenda. "I'll show you the grounds, if you like," Melinda said hesitantly.

"Thank you. I'd really appreciate that." Brenda smiled gently at the girl's unhappy face and was highly relieved to see a brief answering smile light up her clear blue eyes. "But I'll have to take you up on that later." She glanced at her watch. "Afraid I slept in and haven't even had a cup of coffee yet."

"Miss Sparks, are you an old girlfriend or did Blake really hire you to look after them until Betsy comes back?"

"I most definitely am not an old girlfriend. We met only yesterday, and I intend to do the very best I can to look after them," she said briskly, dismissing the sudden vivid memory of that unforgettable kiss. There was still a droop to Melinda's mouth, so she said, "But I will still need some help I'm afraid. My legs fail me at times. Like milking goats. I've never been near one, let alone milked one! Where do they keep them?"

Brenda was very relieved to see the shadow disappear

from the young face and a delightful grin made her catch a glimpse of how beautiful this girl would be one day.

"They're in a paddock the other side of the garages. They'll be wondering what's happened to me. Would you like to come and meet them?"

Brenda hesitated, and then said reluctantly, "I'm afraid I really can't, Melinda. Perhaps I won't be running so late tomorrow."

The bright blue eyes studied Brenda for a moment, before they looked down at the ground. She bent down and picked up a small twig and crushed a couple of the leaves; the fragrance of eucalyptus reached Brenda. Melinda looked up at Brenda miserably.

"I'm sorry I was so rude to you before, but Rick was so upset for some reason. He. . .he's usually not like that. Only. . .," she hesitated, and then burst out impulsively, "only, something happened to him before the accident. And then he had to spend so much time in traction in the hospital, and then the way his father died. . . He's very depressed. I'm just so relieved Blake is home now." She finished abruptly, but her eyes pleaded for Brenda's understanding.

"You are not just pretty, but a very lovely girl," Brenda said very gently. "I won't hurt your friend. Perhaps we can get our heads together and help him however we can."

The young face lit up with relief. "My mum and dad will want to help you any way they can, too. We've been friends of the Warwycks forever. And. . .and I've been praying awfully hard," she finished shyly.

"Great! And we'll all still need to pray even harder, I suspect. I have a horrible feeling I'm going to need all the help I can get."

"Do. . .do you really think I'm pretty?"

"Yes. . .inside and out." Brenda's smile was gentle, as the anxious look disappeared from the younger face.

"I think you're very beautiful," Melinda said shyly and then confided wistfully, "I wish I was as tall as you and had such gorgeous thick hair."

Brenda stared at her and then remembered what Jack had said. Suddenly, she burst out laughing. Melinda blushed an even deeper shade of red.

"Oh, dear," Brenda gasped, "I'm sorry. What a delightful girl you are. I've just been admiring your petiteness and envying you the lovely color of your blond hair in the sun. Being so tall can be a real nuisance, I can assure you," she added a little grimly, thinking of all the boys over the years who had resented her being taller or as tall as they. Even the prosthesis maker had teased her about the extra inches that were needed.

"You really do think I look okay?" All the uncertainty and lack of confidence of adolescence was in the unbelieving voice.

"Yes, I most certainly do," Brenda said positively.

They smiled at each other before Brenda started back to the house.

"Oh, Miss Sparks," Melinda called after her, "My friends call me Lindy, and that path will lead you to the back door into the laundry."

"Thanks, Lindy. And my friends call me Brenda."

She wondered for a moment whether she should go back and confront Rick again. No way! It had been a long time since her meal with Blake in the restaurant. She needed at least a cup of coffee before anything else.

six

Brenda's first priority, after enjoying a quick cup of coffee and some toast, was cleaning up the messy kitchen. As she washed up and put the food away, she found her thoughts dwelling on her time with Blake the evening before. Never could she remember feeling so at ease with a man so quickly.

She pondered for a while on his comments about coming to grips with spiritual things. Suddenly, she longed to know what had happened in the States to change him. Perhaps they might even be able to talk one day about some of her own mixed feelings about faith and prayer that she'd had since her accident. Then she wistfully wondered if a day would ever come when she could freely tell him about her leg. Her thoughts drifted to his kiss, but she slammed a cupboard door shut on the last plate and decisively headed for the laundry. Enough was enough.

Brenda wrinkled her nose with distaste at the overflowing basket of dirty clothes, and another clothes basket of ironing. This room looked like it contained her first job, before Blake and Rick ran out of clothes! She frowned. Surely Blake had said it was only yesterday that this Betsy had broken her leg. Certainly yesterday had been Monday and in all probability the usual wash day, but this looked like much more than one week's wash!

By lunch time, Brenda was wondering even more about the housekeeper, and even more about Annette Warwyck. Surely she must have known how Betsy had been neglecting certain areas of the housework. Not only was there another pile of ironing shoved away in a cupboard, but the kitchen cupboards were filthy and the bathroom next to Rick's room was also sadly in need of a lot of elbow grease to get rid of the scum and green mold on the tiles. But that would have to wait, she had decided.

She was very grateful that Lindy had stayed and helped hang out the clothes on the large rotary clothesline while she had tackled the ironing.

At last Lindy went home but, after he had swallowed a few mouthfuls of the light lunch Brenda had set out for them both on the kitchen table, Rick disappeared into his bedroom.

He had remained very quiet and withdrawn. Brenda had intended to ask more questions about what had happened the previous summer, but there had been something about his drawn face and haunted eyes that had stopped her.

She propped her elbows on the table and rested her head on her hands. The morning had been a strain and she felt weary. She hadn't been able to find a stool to sit on while ironing and had found that standing in the same spot seemed to make her legs ache as much as they had the day before. Unless I'm still recovering from yesterday, she groaned silently, knowing that very soon she would have to start again.

She had just reluctantly heaved herself to her feet when she heard a car pull up outside. The leap of her heart surprised her. But instead of following the mad urge she had to rush outside and see if it was Blake, she carefully carried the lunch dishes to the sink. She had filled the sink with hot water when she heard the laundry screen door slam and then Blake was in the room.

Brenda blinked. He was even more gorgeous than he had been yesterday. The open-necked white shirt seemed to highlight his olive skin.

In the early hours of the morning, she had firmly decided that the next time she saw him she would pretend that the kiss had never happened. Now, as she turned and came face to face with him, she felt her resolve weakening.

"Hello, have you had lunch?" she forced herself to say cheerfully.

Brown eyes studied her carefully. There was a pause. "Are you all right?" His voice sounded anxious.

"Ye. . .yes, of course."

"I've been worried about you all morning." His voice deepened as it had on the phone.

Fire shot through her and left her speechless.

"I'm really sorry I had to leave without seeing you," that beautiful voice continued slowly. And then the warmth left her as he said, "Please don't think I always leave the kitchen in such a mess. I slept longer than I should have and Rick reacted badly when I told him about you. When I had to leave, he was very angry and upset because I'd employed you. Is he okay?"

She was annoyed with herself that she suddenly felt so disappointed that his concern had been for Rick after all.

"Things were a little rocky to start with, but he. . .he'll come around. Lindy was here this morning, and he's spent most of the time resting on his bed," she said quickly.

"Lindy Wood?" Blake asked.

When Brenda nodded, he smiled briefly. "She's a good kid." Then he frowned. "I'm beginning to wonder if Rick isn't lying around too much, though. It's time I rang his doctor to find out exactly what he should be doing in the way of exercise."

He swept back the black hair. How come that suddenly seemed so familiar, so endearing? she thought wildly.

"I'll make a cup of tea for you," she said nervously, trying to find an excuse to turn her back on him for a few minutes. For one insane instant, she had wanted to reach up and brush back his hair for him.

But she paused, as he said a little impatiently, "No, thanks. I've had lunch. Did Rick show you around?"

"Lindy showed me where things were in the kitchen and laundry," she said quickly.

He frowned. "I'll show you the rest of the place," he said after a pause, obviously refraining from comment about Rick.

He strode out the kitchen door and she trailed after him as he went through the dining room and lounge, with no comment. The room opposite his stepmother's room was a very well-equipped study. It was very dusty, her critical eyes noted.

With awestruck eyes Brenda eyed another computer but before she could comment, he said harshly, "This is as Dad must have had it. Annette left it for me to sort out."

His face was expressionless as he turned abruptly and waited for her to precede him out of the room. It was her turn to only take a very cursory look at his very masculine room, before moving quickly to the next. Rick's room was almost wall to wall posters of various pop stars and movies. It was also very untidy. Blake frowned, but said nothing as he led the way out to the family room.

"Rick and I have always spent most of our time in this room. Have a look around while I have a word with Rick," he said abruptly and headed for the veranda.

She hoped he wasn't about to rip into Rick. She'd certainly get the blame for that, if he did. She almost followed him, but then she shrugged. He was the boss, after all.

As she looked around, Brenda decided she liked this room

the best of all. A couple of colorful bean bag chairs and several hanging ferns completed the appearance of a comfortable, well-used, massive family room, far removed from the formal lounge and dining areas. Very thoughtfully Brenda peered around her. This was a beautiful home. It appeared as if no expense had been spared. There were plenty of well-filled bookshelves and one whole shelf displayed many computer games.

She frowned. With this kind of background, what had happened to cause a fifteen-year-old boy to prefer the hazards of King's Cross? Or, when he had told them that was where he was heading, had that been also a lie, trying to make himself sound mature? Surely he would have relatives or friends somewhere with whom he could have stayed if things were intolerable at home.

As she examined the bookshelves, she noted some old Mark Twain books. Jack had introduced her to Tom Sawyer and his friends not long after she had gone to live with them. Then there was a rather battered copy of *Pilgrim's Progress*. Blake's name was inside the front cover, an award from his Sunday school days. It was obviously an old favorite like her own copy. Their tastes were very similar, she remembered from their first meal together. Rather hurriedly, she replaced the book and went out onto the veranda.

To her relief, there was more color in Rick's face and he even smiled slightly at her as she paused beside him.

"Come on, I'll show you the grounds, too," Blake said.

He waited patiently for her as she made her way slowly down onto the lawn. They began to stroll over to the bank of hibiscus and the high fence.

"Is that a swimming pool?" Brenda asked.

"It certainly is. Dad had it put in only a couple of

years ago."

"Is it used very much?"

"Dad used to swim a lot each morning. We all did. Great fun. Lindy told me that it's hardly been used this summer though. She comes over anytime, but she informed me it wasn't much fun by herself. Do you like to swim?"

She hesitated, before saying very quietly, "I used to swim a lot before I injured my legs."

As they reached the high gate at the pool's entrance, Blake remained silent, much to Brenda's relief. It was the largest private pool she had ever seen. The filter was bubbling gently away at one end of the beautifully white-tiled in-ground pool. Scattered around here also was outdoor furniture and even a small greenhouse filled with many ferns and plants with shiny leaves.

"Oh, this is lovely," she said softly. "Has Rick not been in it at all since the accident?"

Blake lifted the knob at the top of the gate and held it open for her. "Lindy also told me that Dad managed to coax Rick in because the physiotherapist said he could do exercises in water to strengthen the muscles in his back easier than anywhere else. When she found out they had this pool, she persuaded the doctor to let him come home a bit sooner as long as he swam regularly. Then. . .," Blake's voice faltered. "Apparently since Dad died, Rick hasn't been near the pool. Lindy said she tried and tried, until he said he didn't want her over here if she didn't shut up about it. Do you think you might help me to persuade him? You would have to get into the water with him when I'm not here."

"I haven't been swimming at all since my accident," Brenda said gently. "And I'm sure that if you can't persuade him, no one can."

"I don't know about that," Blake answered.

Brenda turned to look at him; he was studying her very thoughtfully. "I think you could twist both of us around your little finger, if you tried," he said.

She felt warmth touch her cheeks and then she turned hastily away and out of the pool enclosure. Pausing after he had slammed shut the gate behind him, she said brightly, "Lindy said you have some goats. Are they on the other side of the garages?"

He was silent as he joined her. She risked a swift glance at his face, and saw his lips twist into a grin.

They went past the pool enclosure and he showed her the large three-car garage. Next to them was an empty dog's kennel.

"We had a collie dog when my mother was alive," Blake said a little wistfully when she asked him about it. "But Annette doesn't like dogs, so we never replaced Bonnie after she died. For some unknown reason, my stepmother stated that she prefers those."

"Those" were the goats. There were three of them. Brenda looked at them doubtfully as they bleated and trotted over to the fence of their enclosure after having heard Blake's voice.

"Lindy said she's been milking them for you."

As she watched Blake stroke the neck of one that put its head over the fence, she suddenly wondered if this might be one of the jobs expected of her. One that Jack had warned her about. The goats could easily make her lose her balance and she knew she wouldn't be able to crouch down to milk them.

"I hope she can keep doing it when school starts again." She hoped she didn't sound as concerned as she felt, but there must have been something in her voice, as Blake looked steadily at her for a moment.

"This was always Rick's job," he said slowly, "but apparently Lindy's been milking them since Annette got tired of it soon after his accident. Annette must have changed her mind about them being cute. Lindy informed me, most indignantly, that Annette called them messy, horrible animals. There's only Ethel here to milk at the moment. Nanny over there won't have her kid until another month or so. Make sure you keep a close eye out for old Billy. He likes to butt people when they aren't looking."

"I'm not sure I could be very fond of them, either. But please don't tell Lindy," she begged with a laugh.

His face lit up as he smiled gently at her. "Well, Betsy point-blank refused, I was informed."

"What do you do with the milk?" Brenda said swiftly, trying desperately not to let him see how that smile had affected her.

He pulled a face. "None of us like it, I'm afraid. Some of the milk goes to a couple of local people whose babies are allergic to cow's milk. The rest just gets thrown out." He glanced at his watch, took her elbow, and started back to the house. "I think I'd better grab a quick drink. I have to go back to Newcastle."

"Did you come all that way for such a brief time?" she asked with amazement.

He didn't answer her, just gave her a lopsided grin.

Her heart melted. He had been worried about her. What a nice man he was! She beamed up at him. His eyes darkened as they fastened on her smiling lips. For a moment, his hand on her arm tightened, and then he released her and moved away a little.

Brenda avoided looking at him as they went back to the coolness of the house. He quickly swallowed the cold orange juice she poured for him.

"I'm afraid I must go. Is there anything you need me to bring home?"

"A stool," she blurted out. There was silence, and she hurried on, "There's an enormous pile of ironing, and my legs. . .I mean, a stool would be very handy sometimes."

"Are you all right, Brenda? I thought you were limping a bit more." There was no doubt at all about his concern for her now!

Suddenly she felt embarrassed. What had made her blurt that out? "Yes, of course." She strove to make her voice sound brisk and professional. Instead, the words sounded tense and abrupt even to her own ears. "I was only joking. There's a lot to do, but everything's under control. Thank you," she added belatedly as she saw him stiffen.

"Well, don't you dare try to do everything in one day, and exhaust yourself." He was frowning as he turned away.

After he had gone, she went back to the ironing feeling buoyant and nowhere near as weary as she had felt before lunch. As the iron hissed steam over one of his soft white shirts, she found herself unable to stop reliving that moment from the night before when he had kissed her. With a deep longing she was unable to stifle, she knew that she wanted to feel those firm lips engulf her own again, those secure arms hold her close to his strong body.

Then at last, as her legs began to ache again, her euphoria faded. Sadly, she acknowledged that even if he ever did want to kiss her again, she should not allow it. What man would want to be married to someone with only a horrible stump instead of a foot?

Someone who loves me enough and is very sure of God's will, a voice whispered deep inside her.

She shook her head sadly. No. She'd decided before she

had left the rehabilitation unit that God had other plans for her now besides marriage. She hadn't the faintest idea yet what they might be. But if she kept thinking of Blake in this way, only more heartache and despair could follow, perhaps for both of them.

seven

That evening, Brenda stood back and surveyed with considerable pleasure the sparkling crockery and cutlery set out on a beautiful lace tablecloth in the dining room. It had been fun choosing the modern Blue Blossom Royal Albert china and the silverware from the enormous range in the cedar cabinet.

Earlier, she had not been sure whether to set up one end of the huge table in the dining room. When she had appealed to Rick, he had merely shrugged his shoulders and muttered, "You're the boss," very rudely, before returning to his computer. Exasperated, she had stomped back to the kitchen, grimly determined that a showdown was overdue for this teenager. The only thing that stopped her there and then from ripping into him, was the increasing awareness that there was much more behind his behavior than teenage rebellion.

She leaned forward and rearranged the ivy and doubled-red hibiscus centerpiece on the table. Then she glanced at her watch and frowned slightly. Brenda began to wonder what time Blake would be home.

Rick had muttered "around six o'clock" to her query about their teatime. She had felt like shaking him but instead had gritted her teeth and made no further attempt to get him to talk to her. It was five-thirty now and she had been listening for Blake's car for some time. She had assured herself it was just so that she could time the serving of their meal but, deep down, she knew she just wanted to see him again.

There had not been many opportunities over the years to do a lot of fancy cooking for other people. So she had decided to thaw out a frozen leg of lamb and roast it with some potatoes and pumpkin. This was one dish she had often helped Mum Browne to prepare. At least with making that in a strange kitchen, little could go wrong—she hoped!

The meat had cooked beautifully and had been sliced and wrapped in foil but, despite all her efforts, it and the vegetables were fast drying out in the oven by the time seven o'clock came. Brenda's annoyance and disappointment began to deteriorate into rage.

At seven-fifteen, she decided she was starving and that Blake could go hungry, for all she cared. As she stood to start dishing up, the phone rang. She snatched up the extension in the kitchen anxiously.

"Hello," she said a little breathlessly.

"Miss Sparks? Julie Harrison here."

"Oh. . .yes, Miss. . .I mean Doctor Harrison."

There was a friendly chuckle. "Julie will do. Blake asked me to ring. . ."

Oh, did he just?

". . .to tell you he won't be home until much later than he hoped." A pause. "Are you still there?"

Brenda pulled herself together but couldn't completely control the disappointment and anger in her voice.

"Did he want me to keep some tea for him?"

"Oh, no, he's already eaten here. I hope you hadn't gone to any trouble."

"No, no trouble at all. Thank you for ringing." Brenda said very politely. She was certain there was no expression in her voice that time.

"Men are sometimes hopeless, aren't they?" The voice was amused and understanding at the same time. "You must come over, too, some time and spend an evening with my husband and me."

"Your husband?"

A brief pause. "Despite what you may have heard to the contrary, Wally and I have remained very close friends with Blake." The friendly voice was decidedly cooler and there had been the slightest emphasis on her husband's name.

"I. . .I'd like to meet you both very much," Brenda said with a burst of inexplicable relief, although she didn't have a clue what Julie thought she may have heard.

But Brenda still found herself replacing the receiver very precisely. She stomped over to the oven, grabbed the tray of roast vegetables, and slapped it down on the table. She rescued the carefully carved pieces of lamb, also keeping warm on a tray, and slid it across the laminated surface of the kitchen bench. The gravy slopped over as it, too, suffered the same fate. Some of it splashed onto her hand. It stung. She licked it off. Suddenly she stilled. She stared down at the food. Anyone would think she had some right to feel so angry and upset.

"Don't be such an idiot. He's your boss. Has a perfect right to come home whenever he wants to," she muttered to herself. "It's perfectly natural he should see his old friends."

The vision of a short, curvaceous blond kissing and hugging Blake was not so easily dismissed.

"And a perfect right to kiss any of his old friends, too," she said out loud, "especially when they're married.

She jumped as a voice spoke behind her.

"Who has?"

She didn't answer, but started to dish up the food.

"That smells great." The immature voice chose that moment to deepen. "The dining room looks nice. I haven't seen it like that for ages."

"Hungry?" Brenda managed to smile at Rick.

"Not particularly. Was that Blake on the phone?"

"No, Doctor Harrison. Blake won't be home until later." She knew she sounded abrupt, and bit her lip.

Rick shrugged. "It happened a lot when Da—"

She glanced at him sharply as he bit off the word. He was scowling as he turned abruptly and then he disappeared into the dining room. Oh, dear, and she had hoped their tea would not be as silent a meal as lunch.

But despite all her efforts, by the time they had almost finished their first course, she had only managed to coax a few monosyllables from him. Her lips tight, she put out the apple pie and ice cream she had ready. She was too tired tonight to confront him, but this could not, and would not continue if she had any say in it.

"Did you really think I was dead?"

The voice was almost a whisper. Brenda stood rigidly in front of the refrigerator. After a long pause, she turned around and went back to the dining room.

Rick was sitting slumped at the table. As she stared at him, he slowly lifted his head and looked at her out of eyes filled with such suffering, that she impulsively walked a step closer to him.

"Yes," she said.

"But why?" Genuine bewilderment shone from his eyes.

She slowly sat down, not taking her eyes from his. "Do you really want to know, Rick?"

"It. . .it must have been scary. . .that is, thinking I'd been ki. . .," his voice trailed into silence.

She shuddered as the memories came flooding back again. For so long she had been trying to forget. And now twice in one day! Her hands began to tremble and she gripped them tightly in her lap. *Lord, Lord, help me!*

"Scary? It was terrifying!" Brenda said.

"I don't remember anything after the car started skidding," Rick answered.

Brenda looked away from those imploring eyes. She bent her head and shut her eyes tightly for a moment.

"Consider yourself very lucky then." Her voice was harsh, as she fought to control the hard lump that seemed to have lodged in her throat.

"Were. . .were you conscious?" the unrelenting voice persisted.

"For. . .for a little. At first." She had never before been able to put those haunting memories into words, somehow afraid that if she did they would never leave her. Now a pair of dark eyes pleaded to know. They reminded her so vividly of a similar pair, filled with pain, across a restaurant table. This was that sensitive man's brother and he needed, for some reason, to share those memories.

So, at last, choosing her words carefully, she told him about his body lying on her, and then, after they had released her, how she had thought he was dead.

"I tried to find your parents afterwards," she finished. "I felt so responsible—"

"But it wasn't your fault!"

She looked at the haunted brown eyes, knowing they were both remembering those few seconds before she had lost control of the car.

"Perhaps it was both our faults," she said sympathetically. "I was very tired that night, and perhaps Hilary and I should not have pressured you the way we did."

"I didn't know what to do!" Tears shone brightly in his eyes. "Something. . .something had happened here, and I couldn't come home. That truck driver who dropped me off that night at your friend's service station was horrible. He. . .he frightened me. I only went with him to start with because a friend of mine knew him, and said he would safely take me to Sydney. I saw him pop a pill in his mouth once. But he got real nasty when I wouldn't. . .wouldn't . . .smoke one of his 'special' filthy joints—"

The torrent of words broke off. A harsh sob shook the frail body, and his head went down on his hands.

"Oh, why didn't you tell us? You poor kid!"

Brenda was on her feet and around beside the huddled figure as fast as she could. She sat beside him, gathering the shaking boy into her arms. She was dismayed at the thinness of his light frame.

He gave another dry, shuddering sob, and then pushed her away. "I didn't need you then, and I don't need you now," he muttered angrily.

You need Jesus, though, she nearly blurted out. Instead, she asked steadily "Were you really going to King's Cross that day?"

"No, of course not! I'm not that dumb!" He scowled at her. "My grandmother lives at Hornsby."

"Why didn't you tell us? I could have taken you there."

He refused to answer. After a while, she sighed and said, "I don't suppose that is really any of my business now, but we thought you needed help then, and I'm positive you still need help now. Especially when there's apparently no one to wash and clean, and cook and iron, and. . .and all kinds of things I hate to think about." She forced her voice to sound cheerful, remembering the frail ego of young teenage boys. "Oh, no! The ice cream will be melting in this heat."

When she returned to the table with their ice cream, he kept his face turned away.

"I'm afraid our ice cream is now cream," she said doubtfully. "Do you mind?"

"I couldn't eat it," he muttered.

She sighed as she looked at the unappetizing mess. "I don't blame you. I do think it only fair to warn you, I've never really liked housework, and I'm only a fair cook. So don't expect miracles."

"I don't believe in them anymore, that's for sure."

The depth of bitterness in his low voice shook her. She reached out and touched his hand gently. "If there's one thing I've had to learn these past few months, it is not to lose faith, Rick. God does care when bad things happen. I'm very thankful we're both still alive."

"I wish I were dead!"

"You're that sure you're ready to meet Him, are you?" she shot back, and then bit her lip, fighting back other words that might do more harm than good.

She looked at him sadly for a moment, knowing what she had to do. Gritting her teeth, she pushed her chair back from the table.

"Rick, I think there is something I should tell you. Dreadful things have happened to me because of the accident, too, but not once did I really wish I'd been killed."

"But the men who took me in the helicopter to Sydney assured me you'd only broken your legs. I know you're still limping, but they will be okay, won't they?"

"I'm beginning to think that those people around us at the time should have been a lot more specific with their information," she said grimly.

She hesitated again and then did something she had not

been able to do since leaving hospital. With trembling hands, she reached down and started to ease her slacks up over her right leg.

As she did so, she said softly, "Only the hospital staff and my family have seen these. I'm afraid my legs weren't just broken, Rick, they were crushed. The rescue workers took a long time to cut me free. This leg the doctors spent many hours on, repairing the blood vessels and ligaments. It's not pretty. Still needs more plastic surgery."

She looked up at him. He was staring with horror at the thick jagged scar that stretched from her knee down, disappearing into her essential, lace up, supportive leather shoes. She saw him look from her right leg to her left, and the expression of horror increased. She glanced down. The left ankle was exposed, the sock askew.

"My left leg was not as fortunate," she said with forced calmness. "They tried to repair it, too, but it was too badly damaged."

"God!" It was whispered as a prayer.

"Well, He's sure been kept busy looking out for us this year," she managed to smile at his white face. "I've only been able to cope with His help and my family and friends. I'm going to need your help, too. There are still times when I get down in the dumps about it. I'd been looking without success for a job I could do, until I met your brother. Do you think we might be able to help each other?"

"Does. . .does Blake know?"

"Does Blake know what?"

Brenda froze, and then her gaze flew to the tall figure in the doorway. She had just finished covering her legs again, but she looked down frantically to make sure they were hidden. Suddenly she felt sick at the thought of him also looking at her with horror. She didn't realize the anguish that filled her eyes as she looked pleadingly at Rick. He met her glance with a desperate plea in his own face. Then they both turned to stare guiltily at Blake.

"Know what?" The deep drawl demanded an answer as he looked from Rick's pale face to Brenda. "What's going on?" he demanded again, as they stared at him.

"Nothing! Nothing's going on!" Rick suddenly shouted at him as he lurched to his feet. The next moment he had brushed past his halfbrother and disappeared.

"Great!" whispered Brenda savagely. Although she was relieved he had not blurted anything out, she was still left by herself facing the gathering fury she could see darkening the handsome face that moved to a couple of feet from her.

"What have you done to upset Rick?" he asked.

Suddenly she felt her own anger begin to rise. "What have *I* done?" she said at last in a carefully controlled voice.

His eyes narrowed. Her chin went up and she glared back at him.

"Right. What's Rick done then?"

She stared blankly at him. She wanted to scream at him of all the things that had happened to her as a result of meeting his halfbrother. Then a vision of the pale face and desperate plea in the young boy's eyes made her pause. She couldn't hold the angry gaze anymore and turned away and started collecting their untouched dessert.

"I thought you were having an evening with your friends," she said coldly.

"I changed my mind."

With her hands full of plates she turned and glared at him briefly before turning away. "Doctor Harrison must have been upset," she snapped.

She felt his hand grip her above the elbow, trying to stop

her moving away from him. It seemed to ignite the build-ing fury in her. She wrenched away from him and some of the melted ice cream in one of the bowls slopped over onto the floor.

"Now look what you've done!" she said unreasonably. "Leave me alone!" she then heard herself yelling. "You don't have to know everything. There's nothing to know. It's between Rick and me!"

She knew she must have sounded as confused as she felt. His hands reached out and rescued the dishes. The air fairly crackled with tension as he strode past her and out to the kitchen and slammed them down on the bench.

She was halfway across the room toward the other exit to the lounge room when he stormed back to stand in front of her once again and gripped both of her shoulders in his strong hands.

He gave her a little shake. "Now look here, young lady. You are my employee. If you can't behave as such you'll have to leave. I will not have you upsetting Rick. He's had enough to contend with these last few months."

Brenda stared at the dark fury in his face. Lucky for Rick to have both a loyal young girl as well as this strong man to defend him.

She felt a wave of exhaustion sweep through her and felt her body sag. For a moment she thought she saw concern darken his gaze as his grip on her tightened and she tried to distance herself from him.

"Let me go, please," she said very quietly. She felt him hesitate, and then she was free. She looked up at him through a haze of weariness. "I was telling Rick a couple of things that have happened to me these last few months, too. That's all."

The tension between them increased as he stared at her

consideringly. She felt his gaze rest briefly on her lips and then up again to sweep over her face.

"You're very pale. We'll talk tomorrow. Go to bed. I'll clean up in here," he said harshly and then abruptly turned back to the dining room table.

She saw him pause as he took in the setting, realizing the trouble she must have gone to. As he started to swing back to her, she fled.

She paused outside her bedroom door. Rick's door was closed. She hesitated, glanced back toward the rooms she had just left, and then swiftly moved to knock on his door. When there was no answer, she turned the knob and opened the door a crack.

"It's me, Rick. Can I come in for a moment?"

There was a pause and then, "Yeah, I guess so."

Rick was sitting dejectedly on the side of his bed and raised wary eyes to stare at her as she sat beside him. "Did you. . .does he know. . .?"

"No, I didn't tell him anything we'd been talking about, and to answer your question before he interrupted us, no, he doesn't know about my legs. My brother was upset with me when he found out I hadn't told Blake." She took a deep breath. "He only knows that I've been in an accident. I'm so tired of talking about my long stay in the hospital and I'd be happy if I never saw another doctor again," she added rapidly. "I hate people knowing about Ermatroid." She forced her face to relax in a grin at his look of confusion. "Don't you like my prosthesis's name? At the rehabilitation unit we all nicknamed them. Do you think Ermatroid could be just our secret?"

"I. . .I don't know Miss Sparks. Blake doesn't miss much, not with his training. Are you sure he doesn't know?" The young voice that deepened and then squeaked unexpectedly, sounded very doubtful.

When Brenda looked him straight in the eye, she saw only speculation and unspoken sympathy. She warmed to him.

"Oh, please call me Brenda and, no, I think he would have said something." She suddenly remembered that Blake had not followed up his question about her legs in the restaurant. For a moment, doubt made her pause. Surely he would have said something? She shook her head. "No, I'm sure he doesn't. We have a deal then?"

"Does Blake have to know about the accident?" he gulped. "That. . .that I. . .?"

She shook her head again and he suddenly looked very relieved. "Well, I guess we do need help with the house and stuff. Okay, then. It's a deal."

He suddenly smiled a little shyly at her and, although there was still a lingering hint of pain in his eyes, something tugged at her heart. His whole face had lit up the same as Blake's did and made her realize just how much alike the two were. She stood up wearily. Her legs ached and a headache was beginning to throb.

Something she had been wondering about since Blake's early phone call popped into her mind. "Oh, Rick, by the way, what exactly does your brother do?"

The dark brows, much thicker than Blake's, shot up. "How come he didn't tell you?"

"I don't really know. We just didn't get around to that. He just said he had been working overseas for about eighteen months."

A strange expression crossed Rick's face. "He deals with women's. . .er. . .problems," he said slowly.

"Oh, some kind of social worker?"

"Yes. Yes, something like that." Rick suddenly stood up,

also, and turned his back on her. "I'm goin' to bed now," he muttered.

Well, that could explain the hospital background noises over the phone, Brenda decided as she returned to her own room. However, it also lessened the possibility that something to do with work had delayed Blake. Social workers employed by hospitals very rarely worked so late in the evening, unless, of course, there had been an emergency. She paused in the middle of her room as she realized where her wayward thoughts were leading her again. But, for some reason, it still stung that Blake had let Doctor Harrison phone instead of doing so himself.

She hesitated for a while. Although it was still early, she knew she would have to give in and lie down. She had fully intended to wait up for Blake and ask him about the shopping and getting the rest of her things from the flat, but it could wait until morning. No way could she confront him again tonight.

The only nightgown she had grabbed to bring with her was one that Jack had sheepishly presented one evening during visiting hours, not long after her engagement had been broken. It was full length and made from a glistening aqua material. She had managed to smile at her embarrassed foster brother when she had held it up to show him how it looked. But there had been so much love in his face for her, that she had worn it often since then as a reminder of the wordless comfort and love that had been offered with it. Now she slipped it on, but somehow, it didn't work it's usual magic.

She set the alarm clock radio in the room for six-thirty, just in case Blake had to leave early again. Then she stretched out thankfully on the bed, closing her eyes. But while her body relaxed, she found her mind couldn't stop rehashing the events of the day, and the evening. She cringed as she remembered her responses—anger, even jealousy. Mum Browne would have had something appropriate from the Bible to quote about those! She tried to pray but somehow, the words wouldn't come easily.

She worried for a while about having told Rick about her legs. What if he decided to blame himself for that, too? The thought made her sit up. Oh, why hadn't she thought of that before? He was already so depressed, that it very well could only make him worse. She called herself all kinds of a fool. Then she sank back on the bed and stared at the ceiling. There was no doubt he would eventually have found out, so perhaps it was best she had told him.

So will Blake eventually have to know, a small voice in her heart warned her. *But not until he knows me better,* she answered the warning. She refused to think about why that was suddenly so important but, as she fell asleep, the thought was still there on the edge of her mind.

There was something heavy holding her feet down. She whimpered. They hurt. She tried to pull them free again and suddenly there was a man there, and he was looking at her as though she were ugly, repulsive. He turned his back and started to walk away. She tried to call him back. But his dark figure just kept going farther and farther away. She struggled desperately to get up. But the heaviness on her legs wouldn't let her, and there was agony, so much agony. . . She was groaning. . .struggling to move. . .

Then suddenly the man appeared out of the shadows. He had come back. Strong arms reached out to enfold her. It was bliss. She was safe there. Suddenly the weight on her legs was gone and they were free again. There was no more pain. She snuggled into the warmth and security of those strong arms. The dream was so real that the soft material under her cheek smelled faintly of cologne. Something smoothed back her tangled curls and there was a light touch of moisture on her forehead.

Brenda's eyes flew open. Her cheek was resting against a strong shoulder and she could feel the thick hair on the arms that were holding her so firmly. She gave a squeak of fright.

"It's okay, love. Only me." He moved slightly, and the light shining in through her bedroom door lit up Blake's dark features for a moment.

"Blake?" she whispered unbelievingly, afraid to stir unless he was really a part of the dream.

His arms held her a little tighter. "That sure was some nightmare you were having. Want to talk about it?" The soft voice coming out of the darkness was even more concerned then it had been at lunch time. There was some added dimension to it as well, which she couldn't quite place.

"Was it about your accident?" the soft voice persisted.

Her legs! Frantically she struggled to sit up, and he let her go. Had he noticed? A quick glance down the bed showed the bedclothes still covered her. It was dark there, too. She looked toward where she always propped Ermatroid and was thankful to see it was still covered by her housecoat, which she always threw over it so she could easily reach them both first thing in the morning. When she looked back at him, he was steadily watching her, his face in the shadows again.

"I know I'm not supposed to say this, but are you all right, Brenda?" There was a faint gleam of white teeth and a hint of amusement in the deep, mellow voice.

"Yes." she gulped. Her voice was very shaky.

A gentle hand smoothed back the hair from her forehead

and she sat there stunned, unable to say a word, as a soft white handkerchief mopped up the wetness on her face. She hadn't even realized she'd been crying.

"I was just coming past your door on the way to bed, when you screamed." He stopped abruptly, his voice husky. "Really scared me."

"I'm sorry," she managed softly.

He reached over and picked up her trembling hand that was playing with the edge of the sheet and remained silent as he held it firmly in his strong clasp.

She looked down at their linked hands. "I've had nightmares ever since the accident," she admitted reluctantly, "Although it's been a few months since the last time. I thought I'd gotten over them."

"Did something happen today to trigger it off? Was it something you and Rick were talking about?"

She stiffened and withdrew her hand. His voice had been quiet and expressionless, perhaps too much so.

"I think I may have done a bit too much," she said stiltedly. "I was pretty tired when I went to bed. What time is it now?"

"It's only just after eleven."

Annoyance had started to creep into his voice and she felt the tension flow between them again, bringing with it the memory of their angry words in the dining room.

Before she could say anything, he stood up so quickly from the side of the bed that she jumped as the mattress sprang back. Both of his hands were propped on his hips as he stared down at her. His face was still in the shadows, but his body seemed tense.

"Why did you do so much? I noticed the difference in the kitchen and the pile of dirty washing has gone. I thought I told you to take it easy today."

He wasn't just annoyed. Although his voice was tightly controlled, by the time he had finished speaking she knew he was furious.

"I don't really know," she admitted in a small voice, after a considerable pause while she had tried to find a reason. There wasn't any, at least none that she would admit to, even to herself.

His hand moved. With a little shock, she realized how familiar that combing back of his hair had become. She heard him sigh.

"We'll talk about it in the morning," he said in a gentler, carefully controlled voice. "You'll find it hard to go back to sleep. I'll be back in a moment."

Before she could protest, he had disappeared. She sank back onto her pillow, her mind in a turmoil. He was right. Usually she was too afraid of the horror coming back if she went to bed again right away. It had happened a few times while she was still in the hospital. There was a bottle of sleeping tablets at the flat that she had refused to take now for weeks. There had been too many pills since the accident. She closed her eyes and memories of the horror were there. And there was always the smell, the smell of dirt and blood. Television could show the dirt and the blood, she had thought many times since the accident, but never the smell.

When Blake returned, the tears were rolling slowly down her cheeks again. He didn't turn the light on, for which she was very thankful. There was a cup in one of his hands, which he held out to her.

As she sat up, he said, "This is hot milk and some—" He bit off the rest of his words as he saw the light glistening on her face.

The cup went down onto the bedside table. He pulled her

up and the strength of his gesture caused her to fall against him as his arms reached out to cradle her against his chest once more.

"I've made you cry again," he said regretfully. "I'm sorry."

"No," she sniffed, and felt the handkerchief pressed into her hand. "It's just the. . .the dream. . .it's so horrible, I . . ." She battled for control, as he gently rocked her, and murmured soothing words as a mother would to a distraught child.

"It's okay, Brenda. It's okay. Jesus knows all about it. All the pain, the memories. He's here with us. Right now. . ."

Slowly she felt the tension begin to flow out of her as the reality of his words seeped in. How easily she forgot. So many times during these rotten months, she had reached out to find that He *was* there. The bliss she had found in her dream returned, and she moved closer still to the source of physical warmth and comfort.

His hold tightened and suddenly she experienced a different type of tension, one which she felt he shared. She stirred, and his hands moved to her shoulders and gently pushed her away from him so he could see her face.

"Brennie, I think you'd better drink your milk and take these tablets, before I. . ." His voice shook. He trailed a finger across her top lip as he had last night before he kissed her. Her mouth opened of its own volition. He gave a faint groan and she raised her head slightly and their lips melded together.

Those warm firm lips seemed so familiar and she sighed, without realizing it, as though she had come home at last. Her longing to touch him could not be denied. She struggled for a moment to try and free her hands that were pressed so tightly between their bodies. He murmured something that sounded like a protest, but he loosened his arms a little and then her hands were sliding up over the soft hair on his bare forearms, up over firm muscles, until at last they were at the back of his neck and sliding up into the stronger hair on his head.

He nestled her closer. For a moment her lips felt bereft as he moved.

Dear God, she suddenly prayed, *what am I doing?*

She wrenched herself away from him. "No! No! What are you doing?"

"Kissing you," his dazed voice replied. "I. . .I think," he added.

His dark hair brushed her face and his lips slid over her lips again. All resistance melted again and she gave in to the powerful urge to hold him closer. A deep sob welled up in her throat and somehow she found the willpower to pull away from him. Suddenly her body felt chilled as his warmth left her. And then she felt cold and deserted as he moved toward the door.

"I didn't mean for that to happen." His voice sounded as shaken as she felt.

And then he was gone. The light disappeared and she was left shivering with anguish in the dark, both arms wrapped around a body that still tingled, longing to be held.

eight

It was the early hours of the morning before Brenda managed to fall into a light, restless sleep. The clock radio woke her very early and she groaned as she rolled over to turn it off. She'd only put it on because she had wanted to talk to Blake, but how was she going to face him now?

She still wasn't sure just what had come over her the night before. After many sleepless hours, the only thing she had decided was that it had been too long since a man had kissed her or shown any real interest in her as a woman. She had gone out with Robert several times before he had ventured any more than a light good night kiss. And even after they had been engaged for several months, never had his touch possessed and inflamed her as Blake's had.

Perhaps that had been because Robert knew her views about not consummating their love before their marriage vows had been spoken before God, she tried to convince herself. Deep down, she was afraid that if Blake had continued to kiss her, she would have found it much harder to stop him.

"Just shows I can never be complacent about that particular temptation," she whispered grimly.

Resolutely she swung her legs over the side of the bed and stretched out for her housecoat. Her hand paused as the prosthesis was revealed. She glanced down at her leg. *This would have stopped him if he had seen it,* she thought bitterly. Perhaps it was time she told him. And if that did stop him? She shrugged off that possibility with a saddened heart.

She showered and dressed, hesitating over the outfits she had brought with her. Because she had only worn well-fitting jeans instead of slacks before the accident, her choice of clothes was now very limited.

Jack had wanted to give her money, but lovingly she had refused because she knew how hard he and Cathy had been saving to buy their own home before they married. Brenda had managed with her Social Security benefits to buy a few economical, full-length caftans and loose fitting slacks, which she had accepted as necessary but still did not like. Her only extravagance had been the pair of cream culottes in a soft polyester that she had been wearing for her job interviews the day she had met Blake. Now she discarded the other clothes and put on the culottes. They at least were looser than the slacks and the rich golden brown blouse she teamed with it matched some of the highlights in her hair. Her hand was slightly unsteady as she applied eye makeup to try and disguise the shadows from the restless night.

It was well after seven o'clock when she at last ventured out to the kitchen. She gave a sigh of relief that no one else was there. At least a cup of coffee might revive her enough to be able to face Blake.

Who are you kidding? she thought. *Nothing will make that easier.*

She was setting the table for breakfast while the electric kettle heated for her coffee, when Rick wandered in.

"Mornin'," he grunted, before pulling up a chair to the table. His hair was still tousled from sleep.

"Good morning, Rick." She eyed him doubtfully. "Do you want your breakfast now, or just a glass of orange juice?" she asked with a hint of censure in her voice.

"Don't bother on a Saturday," was the surly, slightly obscure reply, leaving Brenda wondering with some exasperation whether he had breakfast on Saturdays.

"Do you know if Blake goes into Newcastle on Saturdays, too?" she asked.

"Nope. Wouldn't have a clue."

Well, at least he's talking to me. . .sort of, she thought grimly.

"Will Lindy be here this morning?" she tried again.

"Nope, Blake's milking Ethel."

"He's already up then?"

She busied herself getting out some peanut butter and jelly from the cupboard to put on the table, carefully keeping her face averted from him. She had felt it flood with color at the mention of Blake's name.

"Brenda," Rick said.

There was some element in the uneven voice that had her eyes flying to his face. His head was averted and he was sitting rigidly at the table, with his hands in his lap.

"Did. . .did you and Blake have a fight last night?"

"What makes you ask that?" she said sharply.

He raised his eyes. They were full of suspicion and dislike. "I heard him down at the pool at dawn. He swam for ages. He only ever used to swim that much when he was really upset about something." He paused, and then swallowed quickly before asking, "Did you tell him about me and the accident?"

Blake was upset? The thrill of delight died a quick death. It couldn't be because he had felt the same longings as herself, as her traitorous heart had first thought!

"No, no of course not," She said quickly, immediately putting aside the thought that she had practically decided this morning she would have to tell him. It could be difficult doing so without involving Rick. "I don't break my promises."

"Don't give me that," he sneered. "All women break their promises."

"Rick! Not this woman!" she said indignantly. "And that's a very sweeping statement. What makes you think that?"

He looked away. "Experience," he muttered.

"Does Lindy break her promises?"

"Lindy?" He looked at her with a startled, arrested look. "Well, no. . .but she's not. . .that is, she's just Lindy," he finished lamely.

"I'm sure she'd feel complimented by that!" Brenda couldn't resist. "And what about your mother, she—"

As soon as the words had left her mouth, she knew that it had been the very worst thing she could have said. Rick's face went white and then he was on his feet yelling at her. "What do you know about anything? Why can't you leave me alone!"

She stood there, stunned, as he stormed out of the room. The door slammed so hard behind him, that a small ornament on the nearby wall fell and shattered on the vinyl-covered floor. Almost at the same time, the phone rang.

By the time she had moved and reached out to pick up the receiver, it stopped ringing. She wondered if Rick or Blake had answered it as she slowly went out to the laundry to get a broom. Next to the broom cupboard was a brand new high stool.

She caught her breath. Blake must have made time in his busy day to go out and find this. She ran a hand lightly over the dark green, vinyl-covered seat. It was well padded for comfort and the stool even had adjustable legs. No wonder he had noticed all the ironing she had done. She regretted the hours she had spent on her feet when, if she had waited to do the bulk of it today, her legs would not be aching as much as they still were.

Something must be very wrong between mother and son to provoke Rick's outburst, was the main thought in her mind as she started to sweep up the broken pieces. She still hadn't mastered the trick of balancing on her right leg with the other at the correct angle so she didn't lose her balance. Picking up anything off the floor was never easy for her. Now, with her mind not really on what she was doing, she swept all the pieces toward one corner so that later she could get down on the floor, with the help of a chair to lean on, and finish picking it up.

The door was flung back, and Blake erupted into the room. "What did you say to Rick?" he snapped at her.

"What did I say to him?"

"He's gone back to bed and refuses to talk to me. I heard the kitchen door slam. He slammed his bedroom door, too." Blake had both hands on his hips and stood glaring at her.

"And so naturally it has to be something I've done!"

"Did you tell him about last night?"

She gaped at him blankly. Then a wave of scarlet filled her face. With it came a flood of hurt that first Rick was blaming her for Blake's being upset, and now Blake thought that she. . .

When she could speak, she said huskily, "I don't kiss and tell."

Brenda watched a dark tide of color sweep over his face. She tilted her chin and said softly, "He was upset because he thought you were. I got the blame for that, too." The emphasis on the last word was slight.

The color receded from his face, leaving it looking slightly pinched. His hands dropped from his hips. "I'm deeply sorry about last night. I was afraid you would have your bags packed, ready to leave this morning."

Of course. He would be upset at the thought of trying to find someone else to clean up and cook for him. Pain lashed her.

"I almost did, but I—" She stopped. She couldn't very well tell him how fleeting the thought of leaving had been before she had dismissed it out of hand, not prepared to admit any reason, even to herself. Her glance slid away from his and down to the pile of rubbish in front of the broom.

"But you need the job," Blake said after a long pause. "Brenda, I'm not sure just what happened last night between us."

He stopped and she dared not look him in the eye. If he didn't know, she thought a little hysterically, then she sure wasn't going to tell him that what had happened had been the pair of them kissing and coming close to completely giving in to temptation.

She felt herself beginning to tremble as he continued. The rich tones had deepened even farther, but he sounded strained as he said, "I can only assure you, I don't make a habit of pouncing on women as I seem to have the last two nights with you. Especially since I've committed my life to Christ. I. . .I've already put it right with Him. I can only ask for your forgiveness."

Brenda stared at him silently, suddenly very ashamed as she thought of all her own failures as a Christian the past few days. And she hadn't gotten around herself to really "putting it right" as he put it.

Blake mistook her silence and bit out, "Rick and I still need you here."

She hid her face from him and began sweeping at the pile of debris again, trying to control her trembling hands.

Should she take this opportunity to leave?

"Brenda, please!" He sounded impatient, and then he added with surprise, "Why are you sweeping that right across the kitchen instead of—" He stopped abruptly as her eyes flew to his face. "Of course," he said stiffly, "the bin's over there. Now, please, say you will stay."

Her eyes searched his. Any emotion always darkened those brown eyes she knew, but this time, they showed little expression except deep concern that she might not stay.

"Blake, I can't stay if I'm going to be on edge wondering when you might kiss me," she said, wishing she could control the shakiness in her voice.

A brief expression flashed across his face so swiftly that she couldn't tell if it was relief or dismay.

"I won't touch you again." His eyes bored into hers, searching them intently. She couldn't look away and she felt the warmth flood into her cheeks as he said so softly she could only just hear, "Until you touch me first."

He was almost to the door, with her staring after him, before she recovered enough to say, "Blake, about Rick."

He stopped and turned to her, one eyebrow lifted.

"I mentioned his mother after he had just accused all women of never keeping promises," she stammered. Blake stiffened, an arrested look on his face. She gestured helplessly with her hands, "He just exploded, and stormed out."

"I'll try and talk to him," he said abruptly and then walked past her into the laundry.

When he returned with a dustpan, he ignored her startled protest. His lips were a tight line in his grim face and further protests died on her lips as he very efficiently swept up the fragments. Still without a word, he emptied the dustpan, thrust it and the broom into her nerveless hands, and

strode out of the room. She stared at the empty doorway
he had disappeared through, and at last a very tender smile
relaxed her lips as the picture filled her heart of that tall,
strong man crouched at her feet.

Whatever he said to Rick was so effective that when
they appeared a while later for breakfast, Rick apologized
and was at least polite as they started eating.

They had almost finished, before Brenda plucked up the
courage to say, "Blake, if you aren't going to be too busy
today, I really will have to go back to the flat."

The disappointment and dismay that unexpectedly filled
Blake's face secretly thrilled her, as she realized what he
was thinking.

"I need to get more of my clothes," she continued swiftly.
"You said you would take me back. We also need to shop
for some food. Milk, bread, fresh fruit. . ."

Blake was smiling at her so warmly, the words dried up.

"Make out a list for me and I can go shopping while you
pack." He turned to Rick. "And you can keep me company
and make sure I don't buy too many specials," he said
firmly.

"I don't feel like going out," said Rick.

"Nevertheless, you're coming. A trip away from here
will do you good." Rick's face darkened but before he could
speak, Blake added very firmly, "I had a talk with your
doctor yesterday and he said there shouldn't be any reason
why you can't start school when it commences. And you
haven't left this place since I arrived home. Now, what
time can you be ready, Brenda?"

Brenda wasn't really surprised when later she was sitting beside Blake in the Holden, with a sullen teenager
lolling in the back. There was a quiet authority about Blake
that would ensure he got his own way in most things.

During the trip, they kept up a quiet conversation, Blake commenting on several changes in the countryside since he had left Australia. After a couple of leading questions from Brenda, he began talking about a trip he had made to Switzerland. He gave a secret thumbs up sign to Brenda when Rick at last asked a question and began showing some interest in Blake's travels. When the car pulled up in front of Jack's flat, all three were relaxed and enjoying themselves.

Then Blake began scowling when he looked at Brenda. "Will Jack be home?" he asked abruptly as she opened her door.

"No, he'll still be on the road. He's an interstate truck driver," she answered cheerfully. "I shouldn't be long."

Blake's expression lightened. "We'll be back within the hour," he promised, before waving goodbye.

For a moment Brenda stared after the car as it disappeared down the street. Blake had sounded as though he minded if she saw Jack! She shrugged. He knew she thought of Jack as her brother, but she suddenly remembered the tension between the two men. Thoughtfully, she turned toward the house.

The rooms seemed stuffy and cramped after the spaciousness of the other house. She opened a couple of windows and left the front door propped open before she started to sort out her clothes.

Brenda picked up a photograph of her nurse's graduation. What a darling Mum Browne was as she beamed proudly beside her. Jack looked very much like his father in this photo, she thought sadly as she looked at the man who had always been quietly in the background but so solid in his faith that love seemed to ooze from him. He had been the stay and support for them all.

She placed the photo carefully on the bottom of the case, before packing her things. She spent some time tidying and cleaning up the flat and then remembered her dirty clothes.

She was in the small bathroom, throwing them into a plastic bag to take with her, when she heard a light rap on the screen door. Before she could call out, she heard it squeak as someone came into the flat. She frowned, realizing she had forgotten to lock the door, and then smiled slightly.

"Is that you, Doug?" she called. "I'll be there in a minute."

"I'm not Doug," said a very unwelcome voice behind her.

She froze and then stiffly swung around to face one of Doug's roommates from next door. Fear leaped up as she saw the expression on his face.

nine

With a tremendous effort of will, Brenda calmly stared back at him. "Isn't it usual to knock and then wait to be admitted?" she said in her best professional voice, as though dealing with a recalcitrant patient.

"Never when I know how welcome I'll be," the man sneered. "Dougie's always been welcome, especially when Jack's away. And now the man you've been shacked up with the past two days has left you here, I'm sure I'll be welcome, too."

The innuendo is his voice and face sickened her. "No! You're not at all welcome, Mr. Stack. Now, please leave."

He stepped back from the bathroom door a step and gave a mock bow. She eyed the distance between him and the doorway. Although she didn't like the thought of being so close to him, it would be better than staying in the small room, so she held the bundle of clothes in front of her and pushed past him into the lounge room. He made no effort to stop her and, in the center of the room, she swung around to face him. He was right behind her.

Before she could retreat, his arms dragged her up against him. "Mr. Stack?" he said. "Now, that's not very friendly. Especially when you're so friendly to me mate, Dougie. Filling him up with all that religious garbage. You know me name's Fred."

He was almost a head shorter than she and, as she stared down at his face, her fear increased. His face was twisted with burning lust, but his eyes. . . Her training noted the pinpoint pupils. His drugged mind could not be reasoned with.

Inwardly, she screamed to God for strength, help. Outwardly, she knew she mustn't show him how frightened she was.

"Let me go, please," she said firmly, and hoped he did not notice the slight tremor she could not control.

"Oh, no, Miss High-and-Mighty," he smirked. "Sure are high, aren't you? So tall, you look down on me." His smirk disappeared and anger filled his face. One of his hands moved behind her back and thrust her painfully up against him. She tried to twist away and was thrown off balance, one arm trapped between their bodies and the other held tightly as he moved his full, moist lips toward her.

A scream tore out of her throat and she was struggling so furiously that she didn't hear the screen door flung back. The man's head went up, and then she was free, falling helplessly to the floor. There was a scuffle, and then a sound of knuckles connecting with the man's jaw.

"Rick! See to Brenda!" roared Blake's voice.

Rick was already beside her, helping her to her knees and letting her use him to lever herself up off the floor.

"What goin' on?" said Doug's anxious voice. "Brenda! You okay?"

"No thanks to this mongrel, if she is!" said Blake furiously. "Here! Give me a hand!"

Doug grabbed Fred's other side and between them they bundled him outside.

Reaction was setting in and Brenda began to shake violently. Rick was helping her across to the lounge when Blake came back. He picked her quivering form up in his arms and sat down with her cradled tightly on his lap.

"Make a hot drink with plenty of sugar for Brenda," he

rapped at Rick. His grip tightened on her and she felt him trembling. "Did he hurt you?"

"No," she managed, trying desperately to control the shudders rippling through her. "I felt so helpless," she gasped, and then burst into tears.

His arms felt blessedly familiar as he comforted her as he had the night before. Then he was sitting her up, mopping up her face, and holding the steaming cup Rick had prepared.

"Yuk!" she exclaimed after one sip, her teeth clattering slightly against the edge of the cup. It was strong tea, heavily laced with sugar.

"Drink it," Blake said firmly.

So she forced it down and even managed a smile at Rick's worried face. "Thank you, Rick," she said softly as the shivering slowly eased. She looked up at Blake's white face. "Perhaps you could pour one for Blake, too," she said. "Only, perhaps he doesn't need quite as much sugar," she teased gently and was relieved to see the strained look in his eyes lessen slightly.

"Boy, Blake, that was a beauty of a king hit," said Rick. His voice was full of admiration but Blake must have felt the quiver that she could not control.

He frowned a warning at Rick as he said, "I think that cup of tea's a good idea. But I'd better see if that excuse for a man is okay." He looked doubtfully at Brenda. "What about the police? Do you think. . .?"

"No," she said slowly after a moment, looking at him pleadingly. "If I was staying here, I'd ring them. But I just want to forget about it now." She hesitated, wondering what his reaction would be, but decided it was only fair to tell him. "I've been suspicious for a while, but today I noticed his eyes. He's on some kind of drug, Blake. He needs help.

If the police come, Doug may be in trouble, too. He's a good kid. I just wish he could get away from those creeps."

"I noticed the man's eyes, too," said Blake abruptly. He held Brenda up for a moment so he could slide away from her and then he stood up. One hand smoothed his hair back. "I'll be back as soon as I can."

As soon as he had disappeared, Brenda held out her almost empty cup to Rick. "Would you mind making a cup of instant coffee for me?" she begged. "I hate tea."

Rick grinned. "And don't tell Blake, huh?"

She grinned back at him.

"Okay," he laughed, "my lips are sealed."

She had finished the coffee before Blake returned. Doug was with him.

"Man, I'm sorry, Brennie," he said. "You okay?"

"Probably a couple of bruises tomorrow, but otherwise no damage, only to my pride," she smiled at him.

"He's really not himself today," Doug said awkwardly.

"Doug, don't you think you could find better accommodations than sharing with those two?" she asked anxiously.

"I've tried," he admitted and than glared at them each in turn. "I can't stand those two. It's been a bit better since you moved into Jack's flat. Jack's hardly ever home, but you always made me welcome, and I could get away over here. But it's just about impossible to get anything I can afford on an apprentice's pay now. At least near to my work. Can't afford much on transport," he said defensively.

"What's your full name and where do you work?" asked Blake thoughtfully.

Doug told him and then he moved toward the door. "Well, guess I'd better go and help his mate with him," he muttered. "See ya."

"Thanks, Doug," Brenda called out as he opened the

door.

"No sweat," he replied, giving her his sweet grin.

After he had gone, it was Rick who broke the short silence. "Blake, couldn't you—"

"I don't know," interrupted Blake, a slight frown creasing his brow.

Rick hesitated and then closed his mouth firmly as he looked at Blake. Brenda glanced back at Blake but he turned away.

"Are you packed?" he asked her tersely. When she nodded, he said, "Well, let's get out of here."

As they carried her belongings out to the car, they made her remain on the lounge. When Blake returned a few minutes later, he looked thoughtfully at her. "Sure that's everything?"

"Yes," she said a little defensively. "Most of my stuff is still in Sydney. Oh, there's my dirty clothes." She pointed to the bag she had dropped when Fred had grabbed her. "I was in the bathroom getting them when. . .," her voice trembled again and she gulped back the memory of her terror.

"Well, let's go."

Blake was beside her, holding out both hands. She let him pull her up. He didn't release her for a moment and they stood close together, exploring each other's eyes. His were very gentle. They dropped to her lips and then he gave a sigh and let go of her hands. He looked back at her ruefully.

Her hands came up to cradle his face. "Thank you, Blake," she whispered and then kissed him gently on his lips before moving swiftly away.

He was silent as he helped her into the car and as they drove away. Rick asked her about Doug and she told him all she knew about his love for his motorbike and the country town where his parents and sister lived. There had been no opportunities there, he had told Brenda, and so he had been forced to move to Newcastle to do his mechanic's training.

"I. . .I've managed to tell him that God loves him and sent Jesus to die for him," Brenda added a little shyly, glancing at Blake.

His answering gleam was very understanding but he tensed as Rick muttered something that sounded to Brenda like "and a fat lot of good that'll do the bloke."

She flushed. *You need to know that equally as much as Doug, young man,* she thought grimly. She opened her mouth, but closed it as Blake gave a signal to turn into a MacDonald's car park.

"What do you want to order?" He broke his silence and glanced at Brenda.

She grinned with delight. "I love it all."

He looked gravely back at her and then turned to Rick.

"Are we going to stay and eat here?" Rick asked hesitantly.

"No," said Blake quickly. "Think your hamburger will keep hot enough until we get to Blackbutt Reserve?

"Great!" Rick sounded more enthusiastic than Brenda had ever heard him.

After they had collected their order from the drive through and were back on the main road heading west, Brenda said thoughtfully, "You know, during all the years I've lived in Newcastle, I never made it to Blackbutt."

"And it's been many years since I was there. Seems years since I even saw a koala or kangaroo, too." Blake sounded a little wistful.

"Didn't have any over in Switzerland?" teased Rick.

Brenda looked over her shoulder. She was delighted to

see the animation in the boy's face. "Probably none in the streets of London or New York, either." She winked at him.

She was relieved to see the serious expression on Blake's face lighten for the first time since they had left the flat.

"I got very homesick at times," he defended himself, "even for your ugly mug," he threw over his shoulder at Rick.

"Missed the pest, did ya?" The voice dipped to a new level, but Brenda heard the delight in it he couldn't suppress.

"Yeah," drawled Blake, as they turned into the nature reserve. "Of course it wasn't bad knowing I could buy a new cassette and hear it myself before it was worn out by the pest."

"That happened only once," groaned Rick, "and I was just a kid."

With an effort, Brenda kept her mouth straight as she caught the twinkle in Blake's eyes while he asked, "So that means of course that I get to play first that new Elton John compact disc that you bought this morning?"

"Sure." Rick's effort to sound nonchalant was spoiled by the unreliability of his vocal chords again. But he joined in their chuckles as they got out of the car and found an empty bench and picnic table.

No shadows from the morning were allowed to invade their time together. Brenda was delighted with the quick repartee exchanged between the two brothers, not seeing the satisfied look the two exchanged as her laugh rang out at last over some silly comment. She admired greatly their quick minds and the friendship between them and silently vowed not to say anything about the accident that might upset Rick's relationship with his brother.

"I'm stuffed," said Rick at last, looking regretfully at the last few french fries. "Coming to see the animals, you two?"

Brenda hesitated and Blake said hastily, "I can stay with Brenda, if you want to go for a stroll."

"Thought you were dying for a look at a cuddly koala," smiled Brenda. Something flared briefly in Blake's eyes as he looked at her, and suddenly she knew it would be best not to be left alone with him. "Come on, lazybones. Let's go," she said.

Rick eagerly went ahead of them as they strolled lazily toward the cages they had seen from the picnic grounds.

"Were you very homesick, Blake?"

"Mainly when I found out things were happening here that I wanted to be involved in," he admitted slowly.

She heard a touch of sadness and regret in his voice and was instantly annoyed with herself for being insensitive. His brother's accident and his father's death would have been such times, she knew.

Impulsively, she slipped a hand in the crook of his elbow, pretending to limp a bit more than usual. That, too, was a mistake.

"Did you hurt yourself when you fell?" he asked anxiously.

"No," she said quickly. "This ground's a bit rough." Then she tilted her chin at him as he looked at the smooth surface of the path and then at her with his one eyebrow tilted inquiringly. He made no comment, just put his other hand over hers.

The peace and beauty of the bush was all around them. There was only the squawk of the birds and the occasional faint rustle in the ferns beside the path. It was too hot for many people to be in the reserve. They lingered in front of the koala sanctuary fairly briefly for the occupants were resting on their branches, fast asleep. It was too hot even for the wallabies and kangaroos to do anything but lie under the shade of the tall gum trees.

"One day, when it's not so hot, we'll come back and walk along the tracks through the bush. There are several places that used to be really beautiful," Blake said softly.

Brenda looked at him. It would be a long time until the days became cooler. Would she know more of God's plans for her then? Would she still be part of Blake's life then? Sad thoughts did not fit into this peaceful place, she told herself and concentrated her attention on Rick. She had noted how absorbed he had been in reading the various pieces of information on the signs for each enclosure so, as they joined him in front of the next enclosure, she asked him if he had ever given any thought to studying about native animals as a career.

He turned away from the animals and looked directly at Blake, as he said challengingly, "As a matter of fact, I'd like to study to be a vet."

"That's great, Rick," Blake beamed at him, his whole face so alight with pride that Brenda had to look away.

Rick looked stunned. "You don't mind?"

A puzzled look changed Blake's expression. "Why do you think I'd mind?"

"Dad did. He said you'd be disappointed."

Brenda was dismayed to see that look of pain return to the boy's face. Blake was obviously so dumbfounded he was at a loss for words.

"My Dad Browne drummed into Jack and me that he didn't care whether we became famous scientists or dug ditches, as long as they were the best ditches we were capable of digging and it was what God wanted us to be doing. I'm sure your dad would be proud of whatever you did," Brenda said quickly.

Two pairs of brown eyes fastened on her and then looked at each other. Blake gave Rick a slight grin.

"You and Jack were lucky. You didn't know our father, I'm afraid, Brenda," he said ruefully. "He was never satisfied with any of my reports or achievements."

"Blake! Did he say that to you, too? But he was always telling me I would never be as good as you." There was disbelief in Rick's amazed voice.

"Our father always gave me the impression I would never be as good as him," said Blake dryly. "That's the main reason I went overseas for more experience. . .to get away from his reputation."

"What did your father do?" asked Brenda curiously.

"He was a doctor," Rick said shortly, "and never was home. Come on, let's go."

He started off down the track toward the parking lot, his head down. They saw him kick viciously at a piece of bark at the side of the path.

"A doctor! That explains—" She broke off in some confusion.

Blake sighed. "I guess I was more fortunate than Rick. At least Dad did spend some time with me when I was Rick's age, even if our relationship deteriorated later," he said painfully. "And Dad's being a humble G.P. isn't why we are able to indulge in a fairly affluent lifestyle. He inherited money from his father who was a very successful plumber."

Brenda opened her mouth to ask him about his own work, but he reached for her hand at the same time. His touch sent her thoughts haywire.

"Come on, we've got to buy the milk on the way home. We didn't want to leave it in the hot car."

It was a silent trip back to Medowie. Brenda felt very

tired after the restless night and the shock of Fred's attack. She was upset, too, that Rick seemed to have retreated again since talking about his father. Blake's expression was very thoughtful and she knew he glanced at her several times, but she avoided catching his eye.

"You both go and have a rest," Blake ordered after they had all raided the refrigerator for cool drinks as soon as they were inside. "And I'll get some tea." He held up a hand and shook his head decisively as she started to protest. "No arguing. I'm the boss, remember?"

She couldn't resist that gentle smile of his, so she just smiled weakly back at him before going to her room. She wished he wasn't such a thoroughly nice man, that any woman with a scrap of sense couldn't help liking him, she thought wistfully.

Or loving him, that deep inner self whispered.

ten

Brenda could not believe she was actually in church, sharing a hymn book with Blake. He had a loud but not very tuneful voice. But it wasn't stopping him from singing the hymn with gusto!

She was afraid she was going to find it difficult to concentrate on the service. When they were seated, his thigh was squashed against hers, due to a rather large lady squeezing into the end of the pew just as the service was starting. He had grinned at her with a gleam in his eye, which made her wonder if there wasn't more room on his other side that he wasn't using! There was no apparent sign of any of the inner turmoil in him that she knew was rapidly increasing deep within herself every time she was close to him.

The three of them had shared a laughter-packed evening the night before, after Blake had hammered on her door and woken her from a deep, refreshing nap, yelling for her to "come and get it!" She and Rick had voted that the steaks he had grilled were perfect. He'd had to thaw them out in the microwave, because a certain young lady had forgotten to take them out of the freezer that morning, he had told Rick solemnly.

"You mean you men both forgot to buy fresh meat?" Brenda had stated loftily.

"Nope!" he'd denied with a triumphant air. "Couldn't buy cold stuff to go off in the hot car while we had a picnic, now could we, Rick?"

"Nope!" Rick had agreed with the same grin on his face

as his brother.

Something had tugged again at her heart at the similarity between them, even as she had continued to stick up for herself against their continuing claims of male superiority in all things. When she had finally proven women's superior intelligence by beating them both later in a game of scrabble, they had yielded, and insisted she was the only one therefore capable of making supper.

So the evening had been a very happy one, ending with the invitation to accompany Blake to church the next morning. Rick had pulled a face, but she had accepted with enthusiasm. But as the evening had advanced there had developed a subtle tension in the atmosphere between Blake and herself. Once he had brushed against her as they cleared away the dishes after the meal. The flame that had swept her body made her gasp. He had looked quizzically at her hot cheeks, and then frowned as he had moved quickly away. After that, she had been very careful to avoid any physical contact. But the tension had increased despite the determined effort of both of them to appear as usual in front of Rick.

The service was being held in a small building right in Medowie. Because she had slept in, they had been running late, slipping into the back row just before the first hymn had been announced.

From a row in front of them, the familiar face of Lindy Wood beamed at her for a moment. Brenda was delighted to see her and was pleasantly surprised by the number of young people attending the service. She determined she would try to get Rick to go with them the next time.

Next time, she thought wistfully. She was beginning to feel so very much as though she belonged in that beautiful house with Rick and Blake. . .that it was home.

Brenda let the beauty and truth of the words during the service seep into her heart and mind. It strengthened her faith, giving her fresh hope that all the difficulties she would face with her handicap in the years to come could be worked out. Even a marriage relationship with the right man?

Blake must have felt her tense and, as the sermon came to an end, he glanced inquiringly at her. She ignored him, unable to meet his eyes at that moment, in case there was any sign of the sudden fervent longing that had suddenly possessed her.

Outside, after the service, several people came up to Blake, welcoming him home. Brenda noted the cool, professional manner in which he answered them, always maintaining a slight, distant expression. When he introduced Brenda, speculative eyes assessed her a few times, especially from the attractive young women, she noted waspishly. She turned with some relief to Lindy when she arrived, followed by a woman who was obviously her mother.

"I'm so pleased to meet you," Mrs. Wood said with such genuine warmth that it took Brenda back a little.

"Hi, Angel!" Blake's face relaxed into his brilliant smile.

"Blake! Oh, it's so good to see you at church again," the woman beamed at him, as he bent and kissed her on the cheek.

He chuckled. "Careful, Angel. You'll make Brenda think I never come here."

"Well, it must be nearly two years now."

"But, as I wrote and told you, I've started trying to put Christ first in my life now," he grinned at her. "Besides, even before your years of prayers were answered for me, I did go to St. Paul's Cathedral to a service during that time," he added defensively.

"You've actually been to St. Paul's?" Lindy said enviously.

"Look, we've been dying to have you over for a meal and tell us about your time overseas," Mrs. Wood said impulsively. "What about coming over for lunch."

"What, now?" said Blake hesitantly.

"Why not?"

"What about Rick? I'm not sure. . ."

"What sort of mood he'll be in today," added Brenda almost silently. Quickly, she said out loud, "Don't worry about him, Mrs. Wood, I'll keep him company."

"No way," said that woman determinedly. "Lindy can drive home with you. She'll persuade him and you can all walk over when you're ready. And my name's Angela, too, by the way, not Angel," she smiled at Brenda, with a teasing look at Blake.

"She earned that title of Angel when I couldn't get my tongue around her name when I was about three, I believe," Blake told Brenda in the car on the short journey home. "But she has always been an angel to me as long as I can remember," he added with a reminiscent smile.

"When Mum was about my age," Lindy said, "she finally decided that you were too much younger than her to wait for you to be old enough to marry, so that's why she snatched up Dad when he appeared on the scene."

"Lindy, she didn't!" Blake's voice sounded horrified. "Whatever did your father say!"

Brenda had a vivid idea how handsome Blake would have been, even at fourteen. Nevertheless, she started to laugh helplessly and, after a quick glance at her, he started to laugh, too. She was delighted to discover his laugh was full and wholehearted. *Like he does everything else,* was her fleeting thought.

All three were still chuckling when they went in search of Rick. They found him lounging on the bed on the veranda. Brenda was dismayed to see his pale face and that haunted look back in his eyes. His scowl lifted when he saw Lindy, but returned when told of the invitation. He declared he hadn't slept much because he had been stiff and uncomfortable most of the night and that in no way was he leaving the house again.

"Did too much, yesterday," said Blake cheerfully with a warning look at Brenda when she gave an exclamation of concern. "Well, we'll take the car that short distance and, if you got from your bedroom to the kitchen, and back out here, you can walk out to the car," he said unsympathetically. "Come on Brenda, Lindy can help Rick out while we find a bottle of soft drink to take over for lunch."

When they were out of earshot, Blake said softly, "His doctor warned me he has been too immobile for too long and that he should have been out and about a lot sooner than this. It's just unused muscles playing up."

Brenda hoped silently he was right and was relieved when the reluctant Rick was at least polite to the Woods. He said very little all through the delightful salad lunch, which was followed by fruit salad and cream-topped pavlova and ice cream for dessert. As soon as they had finished eating and Rick, Lindy, and her two younger brothers had left, the atmosphere between the four adults lightened considerably.

"I'm sorry," said Blake ruefully to their hosts. "I didn't give him a choice about coming out."

"Don't know what's come over that young man," said Tom Woods with a frown.

Lindy's father had given Brenda the impression of an easygoing man. From scraps of conversation during the meal, such as their talk of past games of cricket and golf,

Brenda realized that he and Blake were very good friends.

"Do you know if your father ever found out why he ran away last summer?" Tom asked.

Brenda froze. And then stared with amazement at Blake's exclamation of astonishment.

"Ran away?" Blake asked.

Tom looked disconcerted and then glanced at Angela. "You didn't know?" he said a little awkwardly.

"No," bit out Blake. "I hardly heard from Dad those first six months I was away."

"Oh, Blake dear," said Angela with compassion, "were things as bad as that?"

"I rang a couple of times, but only Rick or Annette was there. He never answered my letters until well after Rick's accident. Rick wrote a few times that first couple of months, and then even those stopped. I felt so helpless!" Blake burst out at last.

"Your father might have been as wonderful a doctor as everyone says, but he was stubborn!" Angela said furiously. "In fact, he was nothing but—"

"Angela!"

She subsided only slightly at Tom's stern voice. "Well, he was. He didn't deserve God to give him two wonderful sons like Blake and Rick," she muttered angrily.

Brenda's heart nearly broke at the love and tenderness that Blake directed at his friend as he said huskily, "Dear old Angel, still wanting to fight my battles." Angela managed a smile at him before he turned to Tom. "Tell me about Rick running away."

"I'm afraid there's not much we can tell you," said Tom worriedly. "I know that Lindy was concerned a while before because he was getting too friendly with a couple of the hooligans around Medowie. He never wanted to go to that prestigious private high school in Newcastle your father insisted on sending him to. It cut him off from the kids he'd gone to primary school with at Medowie who went on to Raymond Terrace High School. I reckon he must have been pretty lonely except for our three."

"In all fairness to Doctor Warwyck, it was Annette who insisted on the private school," said Angela grimly. "Raymond Terrace is an excellent high school, but it wasn't good enough for her."

"Angela!" protested Tom.

Angela stood up and started collecting the dirty dishes. "You two can stay here and talk while Brenda and I adjourn to the kitchen. That woman makes me so mad I could spit!" She marched off with a pile of plates.

Brenda grabbed a few more items and quickly followed her, not daring to look at Blake.

Angela dumped the dishes in the sink and turned to Brenda. "Blake was away from home for so many years, studying and working before he went overseas, that I doubt if he ever realized how much the relationship between his father and stepmother had deteriorated." She hesitated, and bit her lip, and then smiled a little ruefully at Brenda. "I'm sorry. I guess I shouldn't be talking like this to you." She turned away and started scraping plates and rinsing them.

Brenda was at a complete loss to know what to say. She couldn't mention that she had been indirectly involved when Rick had run away, but she wished even more fervently that she knew what had happened to him that had made him so determined not to go home.

She was relieved when her hostess started telling her a few yarns about Blake, from when the final year primary student had mothered the little boy on his first few days at kindergarten.

Brenda found it wasn't hard to picture the cute little black-haired boy with tear-filled eyes. She didn't notice the smile that flickered every now and again in Angela's eyes after Angela had noted the intense interest that Brenda showed in one of her favorite people. She was only too happy to tell story after story about Blake as they had grown up, even about his drift away from his Christian upbringing by his mother and her absolute delight at his new relationship with Christ now.

The two women had almost finished the washing up when Blake appeared in the doorway. Angela broke off what she had been about to say concerning his grief at his mother's death and looked guiltily at him.

"Talking too much again, Angel?" he said with a smile, but Brenda noticed that the smile did not light up his eyes as it usually did.

"It must have been the fascinated audience I had," Angela said defiantly.

Brenda felt a wave of embarrassment sweep over her. Avoiding Blake's suddenly intent look, she dropped the last of the cutlery she had been drying into the drawer.

"I think it's time to go, Brenda. We'd better let Rick lie down again, I guess," he said abruptly before disappearing.

As Brenda self-consciously looked up at Angela, the two women heard him calling out for Rick.

"You blush very charmingly, Brenda. And Blake thought so, too," Angela said seriously. "But don't hurt him, my dear. There's been too much of that in his life from women. He was engaged once you know." Her eyes filled with dismay. "Please, I didn't mean to upset you."

Engaged? Blake, too, knew what it was like to have a broken engagemenet? she thought.

"Would. . .would that have been Julie Harrison that Blake was engaged to?" Brenda asked.

Angela said softly, "Yes, she married one of his best friends."

Blake called out, "Coming Brenda?"

Brenda blinked back the sudden tears that had filled her eyes. "I only wish I had the power to hurt him, because I never could. He. . .he's more likely to hurt me," she heard herself say sadly, only realizing as she looked at the other woman how desperately she wished that wasn't so.

Another bellow from Blake made her turn away from the concern that filled Angela's face and to hurry out to the car. She desperately envied Angela's relationship with her husband as she saw her turn to him as they drove off. His arm around her looked comforting and protective as they both waved goodbye.

"Do you drive?" Blake asked as he pulled up in their driveway.

Brenda's glance flew to Rick. He stared stonily back at her. "I haven't driven for some time, but I have a current license."

"Tom's offered me a lift tomorrow," Blake said abruptly. "You can drive Rick into Raymond Terrace and get him anything he needs by way of a uniform for the Terrace High." There was a strangled sound from Rick. "That okay with you, Rick?"

There was silence. The car came slowly to a halt at the front entrance. Blake turned around and looked at Rick.

"Are you sure it'll be all right, Blake? She was very keen on my going to Newcastle." There was a tinge of excitement in Rick's uneven voice.

"She's not here, is she?" Blake replied a little grimly. "I'll make sure it'll be all right. If Annette's not back by the end of the week, I'll take you in myself and enroll you."

For the rest of the day, the three were very quiet. They went about their own affairs until teatime. Brenda had seen Blake digging in the garden at the front of the house and had longed to be able to go and join him but, instead, had firmly turned on the television in the family room, taking in very little of what she saw. Rick had gone straight to his room until she called him for tea.

Their meal was again interrupted by a couple of phone calls, which Blake terminated fairly abruptly. Rick seemed to resent the intrusion on their mealtime, too, and Brenda thought she heard him mutter something that sounded like "Not again," when Blake left the table the third time to answer the phone.

At Blake's insistence, they had continued to have all their meals in the kitchen area. She had agreed with his terse statement that it was more homey than the formal dining room but, as she couldn't help hearing his end of the conversations, she began to wish he would answer them in the study. He assured each caller that he would be available from next week on. And each caller was obviously a woman. If he kept all the dates she had heard him make over the phone, she and Rick would not have his company very much for those evenings, she thought regretfully.

But she was delighted when he later did join her while she was watching a movie on television. One of her favorite actors, Cary Grant, was falling in love in *An Affair to Remember*. She vaguely remembered seeing it years ago and was absorbed in it when Blake sat down beside her on the cane lounge in the family room. She welcomed him with a smile and then her eyes were glued to the screen again.

It wasn't until she felt a tissue pressed into her hand at

one point, that she realized the tears were streaming down her face as the ambulance raced Deborah Kerr to the hospital. Somehow, by the end of the movie when the lovers were together again, Blake's arm had tucked her to his side and her head had fallen onto his shoulder.

It seemed perfectly natural for his hand to gently raise her chin, mop up her remaining tears, and then kiss her very gently on her mouth. "It's only fairy tale stuff, love. Don't let it upset you so much," he murmured tenderly.

She couldn't tell him how much she envied the woman who had a man love her so much that he didn't care about any disability she might have. So she just stared wordlessly at him out of her tear-drenched eyes.

He studied her intently for endless minutes. "Your eyes change color with your every mood. They're very green tonight. Other times they are speckled with golden brown," he said very softly at last. For a moment she felt his arms drawing her closer and then the expression on his face changed in the blink of an eye.

"Good night, Brenda," he whispered in a strangled voice. His arms released her, and he was gone.

৯

After another restless night, Brenda slept in again. She had a very sketchy wash, threw on her clothes as fast as she could, and whirled out of her room, straight into a solid form.

"Oomph!" it yelled. Strong arms grabbed for her as she went off balance. "We'll have to stop meeting like this," a deep voice snarled. "Do you make it a habit of bumping into people in corridors!"

A car tooted outside. Strong hands on her arms hauled her against him, and firm lips, tasting faintly of peppermint toothpaste, savagely possessed her. He pushed her back, supporting her as she regained her balance. She stared breathlessly at him. He looked dreadfully tired. The horn tooted impatiently.

"I left some money on the kitchen table. If it's not enough, ask them for an account," he snapped as he let her go.

She watched him disappear into the lounge room and she stirred only when the front door slammed shut. On trembling legs, she made it to the kitchen. She sank into a chair and groaned as she pressed her face into her hands. He had looked as though he had slept as little as she had. Oh, why did he have to keep on kissing her! Didn't he know what it did to a her?

"Morning—Wow! what hit this place!"

Rick's voice brought Brenda's head up and the first thing she saw was the smashed jar near her foot. Her dazed gaze moved slowly around the kitchen. Cupboards were open; remains of a hasty breakfast littered the sink and the table.

"You in a hurry, or something?"

"No!" she snapped. "Blake. I just got here."

Rick whistled. "What was wrong with the guy? He always blasts me if I leave the place a fraction as bad as this!"

"Who knows!" Under her breath, she added, "Or cares!"

Rick walked around the table and sat down opposite her. She glared at him. One of his eyebrow was cocked inquiringly. It made her angrier. He had no right to look so much like that. . .that. . .

"We going shopping, first thing?" he asked hesitantly. Before she could answer, he burst out, "I don't know what she'll say."

She focused on him slowly. "Who?"

"My moth—Ann," he said belligerently.

She stood up, dodged the mess on the floor, and headed

for the electric kettle. "If Blake says not to worry about her, you needn't."

The last thing she felt like doing was shopping—or driving a car. It had been dread of that, as well as thinking about any possibility of a relationship with Blake, that had kept her awake most of the night. And now he had gone before she could tell him she wouldn't, couldn't drive!

"Reckon we can go straight after breakfast?"

"Where?"

"Shopping. Uniforms, exercise books, etc., etc., etc."

His sarcasm was the last straw.

"Don't you get smart with me, young man," she heard herself yelling at him. She picked up the electric kettle and turned the tap on so hard that water shot all over the front of her tee shirt. Turning off the tap, she slammed the kettle down, plugged it in, and blindly reached for a tea towel to mop up the water.

"Tsk, tsk, and the lady goes to church, and then loses her temper."

She stilled, grasping for control. Tears stung her eyes.

"And it wouldn't hurt you to go, too," said Lindy's voice quietly. "You mightn't be so hard to get along with. You all right, Brenda?"

People are always asking me if I'm all right, flashed into Brenda's mind, bringing back a vivid memory of the time she had been in a temper with Blake. *But I've stopped saying I'm sorry,* she thought defiantly.

"Good morning, Lindy," she said with a forced smile. She glanced at Rick and then did smile at the look of surprise at his friend's criticism. "You're here early. Milking again?"

"Yes," said Lindy shortly. "I've already done it."

Brenda looked at her quickly. The girl seemed shaken.

"What's up?" she asked with concern.

Lindy took a deep breath. She walked over to the sink and swung the bucket up onto it. "There was a brown snake in the goat's paddock," she said calmly.

"Snake!" Brenda felt the color leave her own cheeks. Her hatred of snakes was legendary in the Browne household. She had been still testing out her new family on that never-forgotten picnic to the Warragamba Dam Reserve south west of Sydney. The defiant act of fooling around in the forbidden high grass had brought its own punishment when she had been bitten by a snake.

"Oh, we get the odd one around here," said Rick offhandedly. "Lindy. . .," his voice hesitated. "Blake said I'm going to the Terrace High this year."

Lindy beamed. "Fantastic!"

"We're going to get the uniforms today. Aren't we, Brenda?"

"Oh, Rick, I'm not sure how I'll do driving the car. I. . .I haven't driven since the accident," she said anxiously.

"Oh." He looked very crestfallen.

"Brenda," the diffidence in Lindy's voice brought her eyes to fasten on her. "Rick. . .Rick told me about your leg."

Brenda flashed a panic-stricken look at the now blushing boy.

"It's okay," Lindy said with dignity. "I promised I wouldn't mention it to a soul."

"But you just told her," he muttered sulkily.

"That's so she'll know I know, so she can ask me for help when she needs it," said Lindy matter of factly. "Now, don't worry, Brenda, we won't say anything to anybody else. Not even my Mum," she finished as though that was the ultimate sacrifice. "And. . .and I'm glad I know because I can pray for you, too."

"Yeah, like you have for me? Don't reckon He's been listening too much!"

Lindy flashed back at Rick, "Like I've told you and told you, He's probably waiting for you to pray for yourself!"

Rick stared back at her for a moment. Something flickered in his eyes before he glanced down.

"But I'm not giving up on you, Rick." Lindy's tones were a little trembly. "Jesus won't, either. He loves you so much, you'll have to give in to Him someday! Now," she added briskly, "what are you going to do about going into Raymond Terrace?"

Two pairs of anxious eyes were fastened on Brenda.

"It's your left leg, isn't it?" Rick said at last.

Brenda clenched her hands. "Yes," she said shortly, still worrying about the pair's ability to keep secrets.

"Well then, there's no problem, is there?"

She looked blankly at him.

"It's only an automatic car. No clutch," he explained impatiently.

Jack had tried to tell her she shouldn't have any trouble driving a car again, as long as it had an automatic transmission. She had shuddered at the idea of it, not willing to admit she was as much terrified by the thought of actually being behind the wheel of a vehicle again, as worrying about the ability of her feet to manage the pedals.

"Do say you'll come now, Brenda. In case she comes back today," Rick pleaded.

There was no need to ask who the "she" was and Brenda found there was no way she could resist that plea. And several hours later, as she drove the Holden back into the garage, she was exhausted, but thrilled. By the time she had negotiated the quiet country roads and reached the

Pacific Highway, her confidence had returned. Raymond Terrace traffic had proved to be no problem at all.

Lindy had regretfully said she had things to do at home. Rick had met a few old friends with their parents on the same quest, and helpful shop assistants had known what uniform was required by the school authorities. Brenda had hidden several smiles at Rick's efforts to let it be known it was all old hat, boring in fact, when his friends were near, but there was an eagerness about him to get everything exactly right that made her heart ache at the foolishness of his mother and father.

Why had they forced him to go to a school that might provide an excellent education but at the same time cause the boy to feel so different from his peers, as well as so lonely, as Angela had suspected?

After they had eaten lunch, Rick disappeared with his "loot" as he called it, and Brenda looked around the kitchen.

She sighed. At least this needed little attention, not like the rest of the house. Lindy and Rick had cleaned up the breakfast things for her in the morning when she had absolutely refused to budge an inch from the house until at least the kitchen was tidy. There was no excuse now not to tackle the rest of the housework.

In fact, Brenda was pleased with what she had accomplished by the time she heard a car approaching the house late in the afternoon. She had finished what she could of the cleaning, and was busy taking a batch of scones out of the oven, when Blake came into the kitchen.

Suddenly the huge, country-style modern kitchen seemed smaller and she knew with dismay that, deep down, she had been longing and waiting for him to come home all day.

But it's too soon, she thought frantically. *I can't be that attracted to him that I want him here all the time. I mustn't be. There has been too much heartbreak this last year. Can I survive anymore?*

eleven

"Hello," Blake said cheerfully.

It didn't seem strange at all that he should stride over and kiss her gently on the cheek. She almost turned her lips to meet his, but he stepped back quickly and surveyed the now-immaculate kitchen.

"This sure looks a lot better. I'm sorry it was in such a mess this morning. I slept later than I intended. And that smells wonderful. Would you like a cuppa?"

She felt too flustered to answer him, heartily thankful that his bad temper of the morning had disappeared. She was glad when he didn't wait for an answer, but reached over, picked up the electric kettle, and commenced filling it. After he had plugged it in and switched it on, he moved over closer to her.

Brenda swallowed and found her voice. "If you want to go and sit down, I can make you some afternoon tea," she said in a carefully controlled voice.

His eyes twinkled at her. "Don't think I know how to boil water? By the look of you, I think you could do with a sitdown while I make the tea."

She almost flounced over to the kitchen table, wishing she'd had a chance to tidy herself up and put at least a touch of lipstick on before he had seen her. She surveyed him carefully. He still looked weary, but there was an air of excitement about him that was making his eyes sparkle and was putting a decided spring in his step. Something good had happened in his day.

She looked down at her clenched hands. The sudden, unexpected longing to go to him and smooth back that lock of hair falling over his face as he bent down to get some cups out, almost overwhelmed her.

"I suppose Rick would like one, too. How have you two gotten on today?" He put the cups in the matching saucers and looked anxiously across at her.

She managed to smile at him. "Not too bad today." She pushed away the memory of a couple of tussles with the teenager in one of the shops. Her economical soul had refused to agree to buy the extravagant pair of shoes "that everyone was wearing."

"We went shopping in Raymond Terrace and I drove the Holden without any trouble after all," she couldn't help adding proudly.

"Whew, that's a relief. I've been worrying about you all day."

"You have? That was foolish of you." She felt her grin must be stretching from ear to ear. He seemed to be making a habit of worrying about her.

He shook his head as though to clear it, not taking his eyes off her for a moment. "And you are even more beautiful than I thought you were last night," he murmured thoughtfully. "I kept thinking all day I must be mistaken."

He took a couple of steps toward her and then stopped. "I'm wondering more than ever if I shouldn't fire you right now, Brenda Sparks. It was one of the hardest things I've ever done." At her bewildered look, he added very softly, brown eyes dark with an emotion she thought she must be dreaming, "Not *really* kissing you last night."

Brenda's heart thundered in her ears. Her eyes clung to him. His gaze seemed to caress her face, and then lingered on her lips. She felt heat scorch through her body as though he had physically touched her.

"Please, we. . .we haven't even known each other a week yet!" She sounded too much as though she was trying to convince herself of that, too! "You won't have to fire me, if. . .if you kiss me like that. I'll just leave under my own steam." She was dismayed to hear that her voice sounded half-strangled and not very convincing.

"Which kiss did you mean by 'like that,' I wonder," he said thoughtfully.

He took another step toward her and she started to scramble to her feet. The whistle blew on the kettle. He shrugged and turned away.

He's just a flirt, she told herself frantically. *You mustn't let him get to you! Think of all those old girlfriends who keep ringing him up, the ones he promised to be available for.*

"I'd rather have coffee," she said with a note of truculence in her trembling voice as he put tea leaves in a pot. She stood up and reached for the bottle of instant coffee granules she had left out on the counter.

"Heresy!"

"Wh. . .what?"

"Don't you know this is a tea-loving country? Nothing like a good cup of tea. Especially billy tea, with the taste of smoke and gum leaves."

"Yuk!" She gave an elaborate shudder. "I found a few years ago I couldn't seem to taste it anymore after I'd sloshed in coffee while studying."

"See, coffee destroyed your tastebuds."

They continued teasing each other while he buttered some scones. Brenda realized she was immensely enjoying the nonsensical conversation. She jumped and then laughed out loud when he suddenly lifted up his head and yelled loudly for Rick to "Come and get it!" Something soft flickered in his eyes for a moment, but he busied himself pouring the water on her instant coffee. Suddenly she realized how very much at home she felt with him. It was just the way her foster father had yelled through the house for her or Jack.

After Rick had walked slowly into the room and carefully lowered himself onto a chair, Blake continued teasing her about her coffee. As though it were being served in a silver jug, instead of straight from a carton, he made an elaborate display of offering the milk she requested. To her delight, Rick suddenly joined in the banter and, before long, they were laughing uproariously when somehow the milk went flying all over the table.

"See, I told you we didn't need a table cloth. Saved you one to wash, didn't I?" Blake chuckled as he finished mopping it up.

"Do you remember the time I knocked over that bottle of drink at one of Ann's dinner parties?"

Brenda noticed Blake give Rick a sharp look, before he said laughingly, "And I was sent out by our irate father to get a dishcloth to mop it up. And didn't we get into trouble for giggling!"

"Yeah!" The smile was suddenly wiped off Rick's face.

"I knocked over my drink that first night at the restaurant," Brenda said quickly, and was relieved to see the strained expression that had darkened Rick's face lighten a little.

"It must be the effect I have on people," mourned Blake.

"Well, it was you who spilled this one," she declared.

Rick stood up slowly. "Guess I'd better lie down for a while again. I've been sitting too long at the computer."

There was silence after he had gone. Blake swallowed a

mouthful of scone, frowning down at the table.

"He misses your father dreadfully, doesn't he?"

Blake took a deep breath and raised his head. Dark misery twisted his face. "So do I. There were times when we disagreed, but I still have to keep reminding myself that he's just not away at one of his many seminars and will be home tomorrow. I'm constantly needing to ask God for peace."

One of her hands involuntary reached out to him. He looked at it and, as soon as she realized what she had done, she went to snatch it away, but he grabbed it and lifted it to his lips.

He held it there and she felt his breath on her fingers as he said, "But I can't help but feel that there's something else about Dad's death that Rick's bottling up."

He released her hand and she put it in her lap, gripping it tightly with her other fingers. His touch did all kinds of things to her breathing!

When she was sure her voice would not shake, she said quietly, "When Lindy was here that first day, she said something that made me wonder. Do you know where your father died?"

"From what I could make out from the incoherent phone call from Annette at the time, he collapsed here at home and was pronounced dead on arrival at the hospital."

"I wonder in what way Rick was involved," she said very thoughtfully.

Blake stood up and began packing away the dirty cups. "You know, I think you may have something," he said abruptly. "He clams up every time Dad is mentioned."

"Blake, this is none of my business I know," she said hurriedly, "but why does Rick call his mother by her first name? I thought you said she doesn't like her name abbreviated."

"Today has been the first time he has mentioned her since she left. I noticed just before that he called her Ann." He ran a hand through his hair. "They were very close when I went overseas. He always called her Mum, or even Mumsie when he wanted to tease her, because he knew she hated it." As he stared at her, he looked very worried. Then he said slowly, "I have a horrible feeling something awful happened here while I was away and, until we find out, I have an idea we may have a very difficult time ahead with Rick."

The sound of the phone's ringing interrupted him. He reached over and picked up the receiver.

"Warwyck speaking," he said briskly and then his face changed. He scowled at Brenda as he said, "I'll get her for you." He held out the receiver. "Lover boy," he snapped softly.

"Robert?" she asked hesitantly into the phone.

There was dead silence and then, "He still doesn't pester you, does he?" snapped Jack's voice.

"Oh, Jack love, it's you," she said eagerly. "I'm so glad you rang."

A kitchen cupboard door slammed behind her.

"What was that?"

"Only Blake. Where are you ringing from?"

"Cath's of course." He sounded impatient. "Does he ring you?" he persisted.

She hesitated, and then said reluctantly, "Robert has rung me a couple of times since I've been back in Newcastle. For a moment I thought you might have given him this number."

"No way! Not to that rotten excuse for a man!"

Brenda winced and held the phone away as he roared at her. A few more words boomed out, followed by an abrupt silence, and then a soft, lilting voice. "You still there, Brennie?" asked Cathy.

She started to laugh lovingly. "Yes, darlin', I'm still here. And I can assure you, I haven't changed my mind about the wedding."

There was a strangled sound behind her and she turned her head to see Blake glaring at her before he stormed out of the kitchen. She nearly dropped the phone as she gaped after him. Cathy's voice was still rattling on and she didn't hear a word.

"Brenda Sparks! Will you answer me?"

"I—I'm sorry, Cathy, there was a distraction here. What did you say?"

"I said, would you please reconsider, and be my brides-maid?"

"Cathy, you know I dare not. I'd probably fall flat on my face."

"But didn't you hear what I just said?" Cathy wailed. "My sister has glandular fever! You professionals would call it mononucleo-something-or-other, and the doctor thinks it will be too much for her. I need you, Brenda!"

"Oh, the poor dear. She must be so disappointed." She paused, knowing there was only one answer she could give this sweet woman who had accepted her so readily as Jack's sister. "It won't be a very graceful wedding procession. And I won't even be able to join in the bridal waltz," she said regretfully.

"As if that matters. You'll do it?" she said so eagerly, that Brenda gave in promptly.

"Yes, I'll do it. But what about the dress? When will I be able to try that on? I don't think I'll be able to get away from here very easily."

"I'm so desperate that I don't mind bringing the dress all

the way from Sydney to you. Fortunately, there was a chance for only one fitting and then she was too sick. There's miles of hem we can let down, and you're so thin, it won't be any problem to take it in, and—"

"Okay, okay," laughed Brenda. "I'll have to find out from my boss what day. I'll ring you back as soon as I can."

A little nervously, she went in search of Blake. Not many bosses liked friends coming to see their employees at work, especially when it would be in their own home.

Knowing that he had been planning to start sorting out the study tonight, she knocked on that door first. There was no answer, so she continued down the corridor to his room. She hesitated briefly, and didn't stop to wonder why she felt relieved when he wasn't there, either.

"Said he was going for a swim," Rick answered her query, without lifting his eyes from a car magazine.

"Would you like to come with me?" He shook his head. "Please, Rick. I'm always a bit scared of slipping over on wet surfaces," she coaxed.

"Can't you wait until he comes inside?"

"No, my friend wants me to ring her straight back about something."

Rick sat up and looked at her with hostility. "Something's upset him. If you want to ask a favor, you'd be best to wait."

"Surely your walking that far would be good exercise for your back, and I noticed there are loungers you could lie on for a while." Remembering what Lindy had said made her determined to get him to accompany her, although she would much rather see Blake when he was in a better mood.

As she went over to the screen doors, she exaggerated her gait slightly. "Please, Rick." She looked back at him, and he scowled at her. "Not scared are you?" she said sympathetically.

He tilted his chin angrily. "Of course not."

"Come on then."

As she opened the screen door, she was jubilant as she heard the bed creak, and then his slow tread as he followed her, step by slow step, down into the courtyard. Neither spoke as they walked across the lawn to the pool. As he raised the special lock on the gate, and held it open for her to enter, she noticed that his hand trembled and that he had lost color.

Once they were inside, her eyes went to the splashing figure almost at the other end of the pool. She moved forward slowly, and then stopped as Rick stayed near the gate.

"I think I'll go back," his voice sounded harsh. When she swung back to him, he was staring at the curved steps near him that went down into the pool. "Blake'll look out for you." With that, he turned, and was gone before she could protest.

"What have you done now to upset him?"

She looked with surprise toward the angry voice. Blake was hauling himself out of the pool. Water streamed from him. As he stood up, he pressed his hair back with both hands and then strode toward her. Wet muscles, gleaming in the sunshine, rippled as he strode toward her. A sprinkling of black hair covered his chest. She had never liked thick hairy chests. His was perfect. And those long legs . . . She blinked as they stopped in front of her.

"Well, what's up with him?" He grabbed a towel and started drying himself.

With difficulty, she found her voice. "Lindy said he hasn't been near the pool since your father. . ."

He paused and then flung the towel over one shoulder.

"It's really none of your business, is it Miss Sparks?" His eyes must have been reflecting the sun, also. They seemed paler, and she had never thought that brown eyes could look so cold.

She stiffened. "I thought you needed help to find out what was upsetting Rick."

"What does it matter to you? I hadn't realized you were already planning your wedding, so your time here won't be as long as I had hoped. Or will it?" His voice had shown just how furious he was, but then it trailed off and, to her stunned ears, it sounded as though he was almost pleading with her to tell him he was wrong.

He thought she was marrying Jack! And he wasn't at all happy about it. In fact, he sounded angry!

She opened her mouth to correct him, but then closed it again. His attraction was far too potent. Perhaps it would be best to let him think she was unavailable.

"My friend, Cathy, rang to say there is a hitch with the . . .the dress," she faltered. It was no good. She couldn't stand there, seeing him so upset. She raised her head and looked him straight in the eye. "My bridesmaid's dress is for her and Jack's wedding," she said very firmly.

She was instantly rewarded by the immense relief that lightened Blake's scowling face. Her traitorous heart sang.

"She says it's essential I have a fitting as soon as possible." She was unaware of the sudden lilt in her own voice.

Blake took a moment to find his voice. "Jack's getting married?"

"Yes, a week from Saturday. Her sister's sick, and they need me to fill in as bridesmaid," she glowed softly. "The dress has to be altered, and she wants to come here to do it."

"When?"

"As soon as possible. I told her it would be difficult for me to go to Sydney—"

"Sydney!"

"So she will come here. But I told her I would ring her back when I had spoken to you."

Blake suddenly turned away and spread out his towel on a lounger. "Make whatever arrangements you want. . .as long as you don't disappear off to Sydney, and you don't upset Rick," he snapped unexpectedly and then strode past her and out of the pool enclosure.

For a brief moment, she almost called him back. There was no need for him to snap at her. If he didn't like the thought of Cathy's coming here, they could always meet in Newcastle. Then she hesitated. After all, he was her employer, a fact she found harder and harder to remember. For a bitter moment, she wished she had let him think she was getting married. His attraction was becoming far too potent to resist, especially if he kept on kissing her.

Shakily, she started slowly back to the house. She took the direct path to the laundry door, hoping to avoid Rick. She didn't think she could handle another session with him on top of Blake. There was the evening meal to finish preparing and then she would find some excuse to go to her room until bedtime.

Although she wasn't the one getting married in almost two weeks' time, she would still have to keep looking for work, because she knew she dare not stay here while she remained in danger of falling in love with Blake.

Her resolve was strengthened that evening as they ate their meal. She had grilled the steak she had taken out of the freezer that morning, and served it with a tossed salad. Blake was deliberately cheerful in front of Rick, with a forced gaiety that set her teeth on edge.

And then the phone calls started again. One made his steak go cold. Then there were two in quick succession, right in the middle of their chocolate cheesecake and ice cream. It was obvious that more of his old girlfriends had discovered he was back.

When the phone rang again, he gestured impatiently to Brenda to answer it, while he quickly swallowed a few mouthfuls. With a set face she picked up the hand piece.

"Warwyck residence. Brenda Sparks speaking," she said in her most professional voice.

There was silence. Brenda said impatiently, "Hello, can I help you?"

"Who are you?" a sharp female voice snapped at her.

Brenda stood a little straighter. "My name is Brenda Sparks. And yours ?"

There was a hiss at the other end. "Is Doctor Warwyck there, please?" the voice snapped imperiously.

Brenda looked hesitantly at the two faces looking curiously at her. "I'm very sorry," she said slowly, "I'm afraid he passed away two months ago." Blake gave an exclamation. "Would you like to speak to his son, Blake?"

There was dead silence. As Blake jumped to his feet, Brenda heard a tearful, shrill voice say, "Of course I know Bill's dead! I was his wife. His wife!"

Blake snatched the receiver from Brenda's nerveless hand.

"Hello?" she heard him bark through her utter confusion.

Doctor Warwyck? Blake was also Doctor Warwyck? She collapsed into the nearest chair, staring with horror at Blake. And she had just told his stepmother that her husband was dead!

"She's the housekeeper," Blake said sharply. "Betsy's in

the hospital with a broken femur."

"Who's on the phone?" asked Rick.

Brenda looked across at Rick. His face had lost color, his expression was anxious.

"Your. . .your. . .mother, I think," she gasped at last.

"What did you say?"

They both looked over at Blake. His voice had risen. It sounded utterly incredulous. As he listened, he suddenly turned around and stared at Rick. They both watched as his face showed bewilderment, astonishment, and then flooded with color, which receded, leaving him very pale. Then his lips twisted as though he was hearing something very painful. His eyes sought Brenda's, before he turned abruptly away so they could no longer see his face.

Brenda felt the pain in his eyes as her own. With a slight exclamation, she stood and quickly went over to him. She slipped her fingers over the hand clenched tightly at his side. He turned slowly, looked at her blindly, and then uncurled his fist and curled his hand tightly around hers.

He continued listening a few more minutes. Brenda heard the voice on the other end stop. There was a change in the murmur she could hear start up again, and the grip on her hand tightened painfully.

"It is rather a shock," Blake said in a strangled voice. He listened again with his eyes closed. "Yes, in two weeks. We. . .he'll look forward to meeting you."

He replaced the receiver, and stared at it for a brief moment. Then he looked at her, his eyes dazed.

"What did she say, Blake?" There was fear in the boy's rough voice.

Brenda saw Blake take a deep breath, as though to summon strength, and turn to look at Rick. He opened his mouth, and the phone shrilled again.

"Do you want me to. . .?" Brenda asked softly, as he just stood there frozen.

He shook his head and snatched up the receiver again. "Hello," he said abruptly. Brenda felt the grip on her hand relax, and a relieved look spread over his face. "Julie! Hang on, I'll go to the phone in the study."

He hung up, strode over to Rick, and put a hand on his shoulder. "Your mother's just told me some startling news, but I'll tell you as soon as I get off the phone." He disappeared.

Julie? A picture of the beautiful blond doctor floated in front of Brenda's eyes as she went back to the table and sat down. I bet he saw her today. That's why he looked so pleased when he got home. A wave of sheer jealousy swept through her. Her phone call was too private to take in the kitchen. And she was a doctor, too!

"Rick. . .Rick. . .does Blake have his doctorate in Social Welfare? Or. . .?" her voice trailed off, as Rick looked away from her with a flush of guilt touching his pale face.

"What do you think Ann could have said to make Blake look like that?"

"I don't know. Rick?"

He looked up at her briefly, and then at the table again. "He. . .he's a doctor. Like Dad. Only now he. . .he's a specialist," he muttered.

Brenda closed her eyes. Why had she never asked long before this?

"What kind of specialist?" she asked feebly.

"An obstetrician."

"An obstetrician! Oh, Rick! Why did you let me think he was a social worker? I feel like such a fool! And I upset your mother needlessly." She suddenly thought of all those phone calls. "All these women who ring him?"

"Old friends who want him to look after them, now that he's starting up his own practice."

"His own practice?"

"Yes, he's using one of Dad's old friend's rooms at first."

"Would that be a Doctor Hickey, by any chance?"

"Yes." Rick was looking at her apprehensively. "Don't be cross, Brenda. I thought it was rather funny you didn't even know what he did. All the women fall all over him because he's a doctor. . .or so Mum, er, Ann said once."

Speechless, Brenda stared at him. Women would fall all over a man as gorgeous as Blake no matter what he did!

"I'm. . .I'm just horribly embarrassed," she said weakly. "I'm not really cross with you."

"You look kind of funny. Were you. . .?" he gulped, and tried again. "Were you angry with me for not staying at the pool?"

"I'm not cross," she growled, and then gave a slight smile when he raised his eyebrows with unbelief. "Sorry. It's not anything you did."

"I tried to tell you! I knew it wasn't the right time to speak to Blake. He was furious when he stormed off to the pool. I hoped it would cool him down. Did you find out what upset him?"

"Yes," she said shortly, and busied herself collecting their dirty plates. That was another misunderstanding she still wasn't sure whether she should have put right or not.

Rick watched her silently and when she didn't speak, he suddenly burst out, "Dad died there, you know."

Brenda's hands stilled at the anguish in his uneven voice. Then, carefully refraining from looking at him, she said softly, "You mean in the pool?"

"Not. . .not right in. On the steps. He was walking up the steps, when he keeled over. I. . .I tried so hard to pull him right out, but my back. . ."

She looked at him. His face was white and full of haunting misery. "Was it a heart attack?" she asked very gently.

Rick shut his eyes as though the memory burning there was too much. "His face went all purple, and he wasn't breathing. We'd been shown cardiac pulmonary resuscitation at school, so I tried. I had to do something! But, after a few minutes, my back gave out on me, and I couldn't . . ."

Silently and out of Rick's sight, Blake had entered the room and stopped dead. Brenda saw him go white with shock as he heard what Rick was saying.

"The. . .the ambulance man said it was a shame I couldn't have kept doing the C.P.R. just a little longer." Rick groaned suddenly. "This sore back! I'm so useless. Just good for nothing, I guess."

The weary, hopeless words brought the tears to Brenda's eyes. She looked helplessly at Blake.

"Where was your mother?" he asked softly.

"Blake!" he stood up so quickly his chair fell over. Fear and shame colored his face, where before it had been so pale.

Blake moved fast and his arms were around the trembling boy, holding him tightly. "It's all right, mate," he murmured, "you did more than you should have, by the sound of it." He was silent for a moment, and then asked again, "Where was Annette?"

There was a dry sob. "She was in the pool, and when she got out, all she could do was stand there, screaming," Rick said scornfully. "I had to yell at her to help me pull him the rest of the way up the steps. Then I thought she was going to faint. I had to yell at her again to ring the ambulance, before she moved." He broke away from Blake and stared at him defiantly. "She didn't really care. I hate her.

She was going to divorce him anyway."

Brenda realized she shouldn't be listening to this. It was a private family affair. She rose hastily but, as she started toward the door, Blake said huskily, "Please. Don't go, Brenda."

"But this is none of my business," she protested faintly.

"We need you."

She couldn't resist the plea in his shaking voice, and stayed where she was, praying silently, desperately, for these two brothers.

Blake turned to the distressed boy. "Rick, that's no real surprise to me, you know. If you sit down again, I'll explain."

"You knew about the divorce?" Rick said as he sank back onto his chair.

"No, I didn't know things were actually that bad," began Blake slowly. "But the relationship between them had been strained for years."

He had pulled up a chair close to Rick and leaned forward, frowning down at the clasped hands between his knees. "But before we talk about that, there's something I wish Annette had told you. Apparently Dad had a heart condition for at least two years."

Rick gave an exclamation of distress.

Blake looked up at him. "I didn't know, either, until a few days ago. When she told me, I rang his doctor, and had a long talk to him. He sounded very frustrated and upset, because apparently Dad had insisted on treating himself. He refused to retire, or rest as much as he should have. They did a post mortem." The sad voice hesitated. He swallowed a few times. His jaw was rigid as he continued, "Dad had a massive heart attack. He died immediately. There was nothing you, or me, or anyone else could have done, Rick."

Rick's eyes filled. "I. . .I thought I had failed him. I thought I had caused it. . .just like the accident. . ." The slight body began to shake with sobs.

Blake leaned forward and took him in his arms. He looked helplessly at Brenda, his own face full of anguish.

"Just let him cry, my dear. It's probably the first time," she said very gently, unaware of how her eyes caressed him with her caring.

He dropped his head against the boy's, and Brenda rose and went to them. She put an arm around each shaking shoulder, and leaned over and kissed each cheek. Blake's was damp with his own tears. Her hand went to his head and her fingers strayed through the black hair lovingly.

Suddenly, she longed to have the right to hold this wonderful man close to her, to give him her comfort. Instead, she forced herself to leave them alone, and stumbled down to her room, went in, and closed the door.

With trembling hands, she pulled down her slacks. Then she sat on the side of the bed, and pulled them impatiently down her legs. The scar looked just as puckered and horrible as it always did. But that could be improved. As she had told Rick, the plastic surgeon had said he could do a lot more for that when she was ready.

Angrily, she unfastened the strap above her right knee, and took off the prosthesis and the thick, protective woolen stocking, leaving the stump of her leg exposed.

Anguish clutched her.

Suddenly, she savagely flung Ermatroid across the room. How she hated it! Before she realized how it would appear to Robert, she had thought she had been coming to grips with the fact of always needing an artificial leg. Blake was a doctor, too! How could she have been so foolish to allow herself to be wide open again to such cruel rejection?

"Oh, God! Why? Why did You let that accident happen? Why did You let them cut off my foot?"

It had been a long time since the first time that this anguished question had rung through her. She thought she had accepted what had happened, come to grips with God's will for her life. But it was so hard, so hard!

She rolled back on the bed and looked blindly at the ceiling. Tonight was different. Tonight the sadness in Blake had reached out to her. How she had longed to give him far more than a friend's comfort! Her hands wanted to wipe away his tears, continue to run through that thick glossy hair, hold his dark head close. She ached to be free to let his lips seal with hers, to have the right to love him.

It was too late to stop the heartbreak. She loved him desperately. How could she stay here, seeing him every day? But how could she leave, while he still needed her?

twelve

A couple of hours later, Brenda heard Blake and Rick go past her room. Her fit of anguish and frustration had made it necessary for her to get down on her knee, and slowly make her way over to retrieve poor Ermatroid. It had been very difficult hauling herself back onto the bed. Since then she had been lying flat on her back, staring at the ceiling.

She wondered if Annette's news, that had affected Blake so strongly, would influence her job in any way. No matter what, she didn't think she could wait until Betsy was capable of looking after the house. Blake would just have to try to replace her as soon as possible or, at the very least, Angela Wood could help them. Cathy would arrive in two days' time, as they had planned on the phone, and Brenda would return to Sydney with her.

"Oh, Mum Browne dear, what shall I do?" she whispered in despair.

Mum Browne was a great believer in prayer's changing things, but nothing could bring back a foot that was gone. Nevertheless, a prayer whelmed up in Brenda for wisdom and strength.

At last, she rolled onto her side and fumbled for her Bible. She leafed through its pages, turning to well-marked passages in Psalms and then eventually to her favorite promise in Isaiah, chapter forty. Mum Browne had firmly pointed it out to her during one of Brenda's lowest times in the hospital.

Once again she claimed the promise that if she waited on

the Lord, if she constantly put her hope in the Lord as another translation put it, she *would* renew her strength. She *would* mount up, soar on wings like eagles. She *would* run and not grow weary. She *would* walk and not faint.

She clenched her fists and prayed fervently, "Oh, God, I'm awful weary. I'm close to fainting. I need You! But I need Blake, too! Oh, help me to wait on You!"

The moments passed and slow tears escaped as she gradually relaxed and a measure of peace came to her.

Then, at long last, she stiffened and sat up. She swung her legs over the side of the bed. The kitchen still needed cleaning up and she desperately needed a drink.

"Brenda, could I see you, please?" A light knock on her door accompanied Blake's deep, hesitant tones.

She took a deep breath, praying that strength and wisdom would be right here, right this moment! But there wasn't much physical strength in her legs when she opened the door and saw his strained, beloved face.

"I need to talk to you. Rick's in bed. He was very upset, and I've given him a mild sedative. I rang Angela, and she'll be here in a moment. She'll stay until we get home. I have to get away from here for a while. Will you come with me?"

There was no way she could resist the pleading in his voice. She nodded silently.

He looked relieved before he turned away abruptly. He led the way out to the garages, through the laundry. He didn't open the garage the Holden was in, but strode to the one beside it.

After he turned on the garage light, Brenda stared at the beautiful gleaming black car . She didn't know much about cars, but she did know that the B.M.W. emblems denoted a very expensive, imported car indeed.

"When did this get here?" she exclaimed in wonder.

"I drove it back today."

"Why didn't you tell us?"

He didn't answer her, just opened her door, and waited for her to be seated. When he was seated beside her and was putting the key in the ignition, he said briefly, "I was going to show you after our afternoon tea."

"Why—" She stopped and remained silent as he backed out the car and drove it slowly up the front drive. She'd had that phone call from Jack, and then he had been so angry.

"Blake, that phone call, it—" she started to say impulsively, but stopped again as a pair of headlights coming along the main road turned into the drive toward them.

"That'll be Angela," Blake said, but didn't stop as they passed, just gave a wave, and then they were out on the road.

The car picked up speed with a beautiful surge of power. It spoke to Brenda of position and money. She slipped a little lower in the seat, misery washing over her. Blake seemed farther away than ever from being any part of her dreams for the future.

"Who's Robert?" His voice was low and intense.

Instead of turning toward Newcastle, Blake had taken the road west toward Raymond Terrace. Brenda turned and looked at him. He sat tensely in his seat. The light from the dashboard was enough to show Brenda that his hands were clenched tightly on the steering wheel.

"My ex-fiancé," she said softly, and watched him relax a little.

"Ex?"

"Very much so," she said firmly.

She knew now the shallowness of her emotions for

Robert in comparison to how she loved this man. And she had long acknowledged, too, that Mum Browne's reservations about Robert and their compatibility in areas of their spiritual lives had been wise.

She saw him relax a little, but his jaw remained thrust forward and the hair that always seemed coal black was untidy, falling forward over that cowlick that formed the peak on his forehead. She suddenly wondered if his mother had pushed that cowlick back into a wave when he was a baby, as she had often taken delight in doing to the dark-haired mites in the nursery before handing them back to the new mums. Would his own son have that same cowlick, that same peak?

A deep longing to be the mother of his son filled her. She dragged her eyes away from his beautiful profile and stared blindly out of the window.

"Why did you tell Annette my father was dead?"

She knew he glanced at her as he spoke, and her eyes swung back to his face. He peered at her again briefly, and she looked away.

"She asked to speak to Doctor Warwyck."

There was a pause. "And, so?"

"The only Doctor Warwyck that I knew had existed in that house was your father," she bit out, trying to control the hurt she still felt because he had never bothered to tell her.

"You didn't know I was a doctor?" Genuine astonishment sounded in his voice. "But what did you think I did?"

She wondered for a moment if he would tear strips off Rick, but she was too annoyed with his stupid trick to worry what he said to that young man.

"When you rang that first morning, I thought I heard a hospital P.A. system in the background, and I asked Rick.

He let me think you were a social worker."

Blake scowled. "But surely something was said."

Brenda had already thought about that. "At church I overheard someone mention Doctor Warwyck to you when I was talking to Angela, but I thought they were talking about your father. Everyone called you Blake." Her voice was short. "I feel like such a fool!"

The car was traveling beside the beautiful stretch of water called Grahamstown Dam. She stared at the light of the moon, reflected on the water, through eyes that filled with tears.

"I'm very, very sorry, Brenda." His voice was soft, and upset. "From that first time in the restaurant, I've felt as though we've known each other for years. It never even entered my mind that you wouldn't know. . ."

He paused. The car was slowing down and was turning into a parking area on the edge of the dam. Brenda had once been taken sailing here by Robert, but had never known how beautiful it could be by moonlight. The thought of Robert failed to move her. She realized there were many ways she knew this man as she had never known her ex-fiancé.

After the sound of the motor had died away, she heard Blake sigh. He reached over and took one of her hands.

"As long as I can remember, I wanted to be a doctor like my father. After I watched my mother just fade away, that resolve became even stronger. I fell into the trap of taking it for granted, like Dad did, that I would join him in his practice. But during my last year as a hospital resident, I decided that what I really wanted to do, above all else, was to be an obstetrician." His long fingers were playing with hers, absent-mindedly. "Dad was upset, to say the very least. I decided it was better to gain more experience in surgery overseas, hoping he would have had time to come to grips with it all."

He hesitated, and looked up at her. "There. . .there was also another reason. I'd been engaged, and when it was broken off, I wanted to get away. I wish now that I'd stayed. There would have been more time with. . .with Dad. And I'd have been here when Rick needed someone."

Her heart swelled with love for him. One hand found its way to touch his cheek. He swiftly turned his head and she helplessly left her hand pressed against his lips as he kissed her palm. Tingles spread down her arm and she snatched both hands away, staring at him in confusion.

He silently looked back at her for several long moments. She turned away, unable to sustain that look without offering him her hands and love to comfort him, as she longed to with every part of her.

"Annette's remarried." His voice was strained and hardly above a whisper.

She gave a sharp exclamation, and turned back to him. Both his hands were resting on the steering wheel.

"Let's go for a walk," he muttered, and opened his door.

She watched him stride down the sealed boat ramp to the edge of the water, a tall, dark figure, slightly hunched at the shoulders. When she joined him, he stood staring out across the moonlit ripples of water, his hands jammed into his pockets. He turned and held out his hand. Helpless to refuse him, she put hers into it and, linked together, they started moving very slowly over the short grass, Brenda taking extra care in the dark where she swung Ermatroid.

"She was married last Saturday." Blake gave a bitter laugh. "Last Saturday! When we were enjoying Blackbutt, my stepmother for sixteen years, Rick's mother, was getting married, without so much as a hint to either of us."

"Blake, I'm so sorry."

He released her hand and slipped his arm around her waist. "When I told Rick, he was actually relieved. He seemed to think she had redeemed herself a little by marrying the man he saw her in bed with about twelve months ago!"

She stopped dead. "Twelve months ago?"

He turned to face her, his hand resting lightly on her hip. "It was why Rick ran away, why he's turned his back on going to church. Annette. . .Annette was fairly regular at worship and was involved in quite a few activities there. He could only see her hypocrisy. I. . .I've had quite a bit to say about that! But he couldn't cope with not telling his father, as she made him promise. So he ran away. Brenda, he. . .he. . .told me about the accident."

She froze, searching his face in the moonlight.

"Why didn't you tell me?" he asked.

She moved, trying to distance herself from him. His other hand came up and he held her firmly by the waist so she couldn't move.

"He didn't want me to," she whispered at long last, "and I. . .I. . ."

"Was too soft-hearted with him," Blake finished gently and then gave a soft laugh. "He's quite convinced that you're the nicest woman he's ever met, he informed me tonight, and if I didn't—" He stopped short, the smile disappearing.

"What did he tell you?" Brenda managed to croak at last through dry lips.

"About the truck driver. About your friend trying to stop him from hitchhiking the rest of the way. About you insisting on taking him home to his parents. His lying about his name and then, when he realized what would happen when you got to the false address, trying to get you to stop." He paused again, the deep, rich tones of his voice washing over her.

Her eyes clung to his. They had stopped under the light from the solitary security spotlight that lit up the area.

"Did he tell you. . .tell you. . .?"

"About him grabbing the steering wheel? Yes." His voice was harsh. "I was close to shaking him by that time and wanted to strangle that selfish mother of his!"

She waited.

"He told me about you being trapped in the car." He gave a groan, and took a step forward to hold her tightly against his body. "I wish I had been there to help you while the broken bones in your legs mended. I wish I could have been there to kiss your pain away."

She held herself stiffly in his embrace. "He told you about my legs?" she whispered helplessly.

A shudder went through him. "He said something about your nasty scar, and that you would need more plastic surgery."

She relaxed slightly. "That's all?"

He released her enough to stare into her eyes. Then he nodded briefly.

She almost collapsed against him with relief. He must have felt the tension flow out of her for he gathered her gently into his arms. His head came closer and, powerless to move, she felt his lips warm and gentle against her own. When she didn't move, there was a strong contraction of his muscles as he tightened his arms, pressing her harder against him. She sighed, as though she had come home.

"Marry me, darling." Blake pleaded.

For one moment, her dreams were very close, within touching distance, as the beauty, the glory of those soft words floated through her. She murmured something inaudible as his lips repossessed her. This was heaven, sheer paradise. She moved to press closer, but the heel of her shoe must have pressed into the ground and she felt the straps around her knee pull.

He must have felt the sudden, utter stillness that held her.

"Tell me you'll marry me," soft words implored her. "I know we've only known each other a very short time, but God knows how I've been waiting for your compassion, your strength, and your sweetness all my life."

She pushed away from him. He let her put a little distance between their bodies, but refused to take his arms completely away.

"Brenda?" There was anguish in his dear, dear voice. "You must love me. You're not the kind of woman to let me kiss you so very thoroughly otherwise, and to kiss me back so. . .so. . ."

The fulfillment of all her dreams lay held in this wonderful man's dear person. She closed her eyes tightly. Then she forced her arms to fall empty to her sides.

"No, I can't marry you, Blake," her soft voice said very gently, very sadly, very firmly.

His hands slid away from her, letting her go. She stumbled blindly back to the car, leaving him a lonely figure in the darkness.

thirteen

Just after dawn, Brenda woke from a deep, exhausted sleep; the pink galahs that frequently perched on the trees in the garden screeched loudly. She had expected not to be able to go to sleep at all, after that miserable, silent rush through the warm evening back to the house. But it had been a long, dreadful day, and she had gone into a deep sleep the minute her head had curled into her pillow.

Stretching, she winced at the stiffness in her back from lying in the one spot too long. With a groan, she rolled over onto her stomach, automatically positioning her legs correctly to do the prone lying exercise necessary to give the muscles that remained in her leg the stretching they needed to keep their tone and flexibility. A gentle breeze blew through the open window, but it reflected the warmth of the sun and, with a sigh, Brenda knew it was going to be another hot day.

I've got to pack, she thought. *It's a shame we bothered to pick up my things from the flat, although it will mean I won't have to get Cathy to go there tomorrow.* She shivered as she remembered the attack. Then she smiled slightly. But it had worked out well for Doug. Blake had found him cheap board with a friend of his and talking about Christ's claim on his life had brought a very positive response, Blake had told a thrilled Brenda.

Her smile disappeared. Blake had not spoken to her again after she had refused his proposal. As she had opened the car door when they had stopped back at the house, he had said good night so sadly, that any more words had died on her lips. She had managed to nod, before stumbling from the car.

Oh, God, have I done the right thing? Wouldn't it have been better to risk saying yes? Blake was a far stronger man than Robert. But could the love he believed he now had for her possibly last? Perhaps a damaged body wouldn't matter to him?

Even if it did, she thought sadly, he would be too kind to show her his abhorrence. And even if his doctor's eyes could look reasonably favorably on her outward scars, other damage done many years ago to her essential spirit made her even more unsuitable to be the wife of this very wonderful doctor.

Memories she had suppressed for many, many years began to surface. A man and a woman with filthy clothes. A filthy room that stank. A child seldom free of bruises, who had learned very early to hide under the house to escape the blows from the drunken swine who had called himself her father. When all would be quiet, she would sneak back into the house, hoping against hope there would be some food in the cupboards.

Then, at the end of one particularly bad period, there had been a horrified policeman on the doorstep. Her mother had been too drunk to understand the mission he had been on. The drunken swine had been hit by a car and would never hit the trembling child again.

Then had started her life of child refuges, foster families, until the Brownes had loved her, as she had not thought possible. But she had always recognized that they were such extraordinary people.

The anguish she had been trying to keep at bay, rose and took possession of her. Her body started to shudder and she rolled onto her side, clutching the pillow tightly to her. *Why am I not crying?* she thought, through pain far deeper than any she had ever known.

Part of her pain was caused by the anguish she had seen in Blake's twisted face, before she had turned from him. From the car she had shivered, as she watched him stride away into the darkness along the lake. When he had returned eons later, he hadn't once glanced at her.

Was it better for them both to suffer some pain now, than be put through the disgust and horror later, when his dreams were shattered as Robert's had been?

She heard the phone ringing in the distance. Someone answered it after a few rings. Probably one of Blake's patients. No girlfriends after all, she couldn't help thinking selfishly, but with a feeling of relief.

She stayed where she was until long after she heard Rick's door open and close with a slam. Not until she thought she heard Blake's car drive away, did she get out of bed. When she had at last dressed, avoiding looking more than once in the mirror at her white mask of a face, she opened her door and then hesitated in the corridor outside. She froze when she heard the murmur of voices from the family room and then relaxed when she heard Lindy's laugh ring out.

Out in the kitchen, she stood at the door and looked at the spotless room, so different from the other days Blake had left early. She smiled wryly. He was hoping to impress her. She shook her head. More likely letting her know he didn't need her anymore.

She found she could only swallow half a piece of toast, but gulped down the coffee thankfully to try and ease the permanent lump that seemed to have lodged in her throat. After rinsing and drying her own cup and plate, she slowly made her way slowly out to the laundry. Might as well leave them with as many clean clothes as I can, she told herself as she turned on the washing machine. The faint smell of after shave on the pale blue shirt that Blake had worn on Sunday was almost her undoing. As she watched it slide down into the hot suds, she wondered frantically if Cathy could possibly come today, instead of tomorrow. If she rang her—

Above the sound of the washing machine, she heard the shrill summons of the phone. Rick or Lindy must have answered it on the extension in the family room. She hesitated as she looked at the ironing from her washing before the weekend. Sighing, she switched on the iron, and pulled down the ironing board. Her hands lingered on the stool Blake had bought for her and that brought back memories of the night he had comforted her after the nightmare.

She couldn't stand it. She switched off the iron and grimly put away the board. She hadn't ventured into Betsy's rooms since Blake had just pointed them out to her on the first day. She still hadn't put away her clothes, so she picked up the basket with them in it and went down the corridor, past the laundry, until she came to the door. Even here, she couldn't get away from the memory of Blake.

"There's nowhere you can't go in this house, Brenda," his quiet voice had said gently, when she had hesitantly queried him about these rooms.

She now felt a faint echo of the glow that his trust in her had produced. With a sigh, she balanced the basket on her hip and maneuvered the door open.

It was the stench that first hit her like a blow, a smell she had hoped never to know again. As she looked around, she gasped with dismay. Because the place had been shut up in the heat, the smell of stale cigarettes, and that other unforgettable stench, were much worse, she supposed grimly.

She moved over to look down with disgust at the moldy scraps of food scattered around on the filthy table and the half-empty flagon of wine beside them. Still carrying the basket, she went through the small living area, into the bedroom, and dumped it on the unmade bed. In there the smell was worse. The carpet beside the bed showed unmistakeable, dirty, mildewed marks. When she opened the wardrobe door, she wasn't really surprised to see a few more newspaper-wrapped bottles of wine. She turned back, her stomach churning as she surveyed the filth, the evidence.

She made it back to the toilet next to the laundry, just in time. When she at last stopped vomiting, she leaned against the door into the laundry.

"What's the matter?" Blake's strong arms were supporting her, turning her gently away, over to the sink. A soft, moist cloth was efficiently wiping her face and then patting it dry, before pulling her against him. "Come on, I'll help you to your room."

"No," she managed to gasp, and pushed him away. "I'm not sick. It was just. . .just. . .Betsy. . ."

"Betsy?"

"Her room. . .it's. . .it's horrible!"

He stared back at her with amazement, before he turned to stride toward the housekeeper's rooms.

Trying to stop the trembling deep inside her and to banish the memories stirred up, she followed him slowly.

When he returned to where she waited for him in the corridor, he looked absolutely shocked. "I don't believe it! I've never seen anything like it before! What was wrong with the woman? And what was Annette thinking of to employ someone like that?" His voice rose, as anger replaced his astonishment.

"I have," said Brenda in a dull voice.

"Have what?"

"Seen something like it before."

"I didn't know you'd done any district nursing."

"I haven't. I saw it every day when I was a child." The memories slipped through her guard and she began to shake. Blake moved toward her, but she fended him off.

"Don't, darling," he said shakily. "It's all in the past, now. Gone. God took you out of it all. Gave you to people who love you. No one will ever hurt you again like that."

She stared blankly at him. You have more power to hurt me than anyone in the world, she wanted to scream at him. Her mouth opened, and then closed again at the change on his face.

"Thank heavens!" she heard him murmur and then she, too, heard the toot, toot of a horn and the sound of a car.

"I can't let anyone see me like this," she said. "Please . . . ."

"These visitors you won't mind in the least," he said with a beautiful smile that caressed and touched her with warmth.

The front door chimes rang out. He gave a laugh. "Come on, I'm looking forward very much to seeing them myself."

Despite her protest to at least let her comb her hair, he hurried her toward the front door. Then she gave a gasp and was flying into the welcoming arms of the massive, red-haired man standing in the open doorway. She burst into shattering sobs.

"Jack! Oh, Jack dear, how did you know I needed you so much?"

"Now, what have you been up to this time, Brennie? Blake been beating you?" There was concern mixed with exasperation in her foster brother's deep voice.

Brenda fought for calm. She raised her tear-streaked face and then realized there was another person waiting patiently to greet her.

"Cathy!"

The tall, auburn-haired woman hugged her back and kissed her on the cheek.

"But you weren't coming until tomorrow," Brenda said.

There was a little pool of stillness. Brenda saw Jack frowning suspiciously at Blake.

"We drove up from Sydney and stayed last night. There was some shopping we thought we might get done easier here," Cathy said gently. She surveyed Brenda's face carefully and her voice was even softer when she added, "I'm glad we did, or we wouldn't have been there when Blake rang early this morning."

Brenda looked from one to the other, her tears drying. A soft handkerchief was slipped into her hand, and she swung around too quickly toward Blake. Off balance, she grabbed for support and felt the strength of his hands grip her and help her regain her balance.

"Hmmm! Thought you would be over that by now," said Jack's voice thoughtfully.

"It only happens when. . .when—"

"When she's upset," Blake said blandly.

How had he worked that out? The memory of a dark stranger's arms around her in a corridor burned in her mind. She wrenched away from him.

"What did you mean? What phone call?" Her eyes narrowed at him, striving for some semblance of calm.

"Let's all go into the lounge room and then we can talk," Blake said inflexibly, turning and indicating to the visitors where to go.

"Hmmm. Nice. Very nice," murmured Cathy.

"Do you think so?" Blake looked around at the rich burgundy leather lounge and the ostentatious units and then back at Cathy as she seated herself. He shrugged. "Afraid, it's not quite to my taste. More to my stepmother's," Blake said pleasantly. "She told me last night she's going to sell this place. Her new husband has a much bigger house at the Goldcoast." A tinge of pain crept into his voice.

"Oh, Blake, I'm so sorry."

Blake looked at Brenda's horrified face. Her heart clenched at the tender expression that swept away the pain.

"I'm not. I never intended living here anyway. We can choose something more to our taste closer to Newcastle. I need to be closer to the surgery and the hospitals. Babies don't like waiting too long."

With some difficulty, Brenda unlocked her eyes from his to see Jack grinning approvingly at him.

"Good. Glad you've got better taste than this, mate," he pronounced. "Now, since Brenda's lost her manners, this is my fiancée, Cathy. And it doesn't appear as though you've done what I suggested yet."

Brenda stared at Jack, and then rather wildly at Blake, as he pushed back his hair and rather sheepishly shook his head at Jack.

"Done what?" she demanded.

"Jack suggested I put you over my knee and wallop you," Blake said. Jack nodded.

Brenda stared at him. The darkness of his eyes and his taut lips told her he was anything but calm. "You. . .you. . ."

"Didn't think I'd just take your words last night as final, did you?" Blake asked.

She stared at him speechlessly. The thought that he had accepted her decision without a protest had stung her last night.

"I found out that you loved Jack only as a brother, after all. Jack assures me you couldn't possibly be longing still for your ex-fiancé." He ignored her gasp of outrage and looked at Jack. "A wimp, I think you called him?"

"That among other things," growled Jack.

"And, as you aren't the kind of woman to lead a bloke on, you must love me." His voice was anything but calm as he added huskily, "You do love me, don't you?"

For all his assured words, she saw the agony of uncertainty in his eyes.

She closed her eyes tightly, to shut out the sight of his pain. Numbly, she shook her head, trying desperately to clear it. Her eyes flew open at the sharp words Blake spat out.

"Jack, please! Try and talk some sense into her, before I do put her over my knee!" Then he turned around, and stalked out of the room.

She stared blindly at the empty doorway Blake had stormed through.

"Phew!"

The soft exclamation brought Brenda's dazed face back to Cathy's rather awed expression.

"That is some man. You must be mad if you haven't fallen in love with him," Cathy said with a sigh.

"Hey! Remember me?" Jack asked.

Brenda watched them grin at each other and a sharp stab of envy lashed her at the security of their love for each other.

"Oh, Jack," Brenda wailed. "What am I going to do? I love him so much!"

"Then why didn't you say yes to him when he asked you to marry him?"

Brenda stared at Jack with astonishment. "How do you know he. . .?"

"He told me on the phone this morning. And I might say, he sounded like one desperate bloke." He ignored Brenda's gasp and went on steadily to say, "And, knowing you, I suppose you think he can't possibly love you because, of course, you are so unlovable, and ugly, and repulsive, and all that garbage!"

He was glaring at Brenda, as he often had over the years, when Brenda had dared to hint at her past.

"Oh, darling, you're such special people," she smiled lovingly, but shakily at them both. "You've always told me I was beautiful. And perhaps my face and body are . . .were. I could believe that until. . ." The rising lump in her throat threatened to choke her.

"You've never really believed you were a person anyone could really love," Jack stated firmly. "We've always worried about that. All because you had a mother and father who abused you, and were too sick and stupid to love the most loveable person we have ever met. And then that wimp of a fiancé of yours finished their job on you, didn't he?"

Brenda gaped at him. Memories flooded back. Those first foster parents had offered her love and she had turned away from them. They had eventually given up on her and turned away from her also. But the Brownes never had. They had seen something in her worth loving, she realized with a blinding flash of acknowledgment. They saw her with God's eyes!

"Jack? Cathy?" she said wildly.

Jack strode over and put his huge arms around the shaking woman. "Do you believe Blake loves you?"

"I think he believes he does," she whispered shakily. "But he doesn't know about my leg. And he's a doctor, and—"

"And you have been extremely foolish, I think. Can't you see God's hand in all of this?"

God gave you people to love you. Blake's words.

Had God given her Blake, too?

Brenda stared at Jack with dawning hope and excitement.

"Give him a chance, Brenda. Tell him about your Ermatroid, although I'm pretty sure you'll find out he already knows. He's no fool. But show him your leg if you feel you must. And remember, if he loves you, really loves you, your hurt will be his, too. You've been hurting for *him*, haven't you?" As Brenda stared at him blankly, he grinned at her and added simply, "He told me. Go on. Go and find him. I think that young man's had enough pain, don't you?"

&

Blake was standing down near the goats' paddock, leaning heavily against a post, his shoulders hunched over as they had been last night, showing his despair and grief.

"Blake," she whispered.

He stiffened, and then he straightened and turned toward her. They searched each other's faces hungrily. She tried to control the trembling in her legs, as she took a hesitant step toward him.

There was a sudden movement in the grass at her feet, a flash of sun on shiny brown skin, and she screamed as the snake struck swiftly at her leg. It slithered away across the grass and she screamed again at the same time Blake's arms wrapped around her, lifting her effortlessly in his arms.

"God!" It was a strangled prayer that pierced through her hysteria, as he stumbled with her toward the house.

"God!" She heard him mutter feverishly again. "Dad, I

hope you still keep anti-venom here!"

He stumbled badly, nearly dropping her.

"Blake!" she managed to croak. "Blake!"

They were at the veranda steps. She vaguely realized that Rick was there and then Cathy and Jack.

"What's happened!" Rick's voice said fearfully.

"Snake bite!" gasped Blake.

Brenda felt a firm mattress beneath her. And then Blake's hands were pushing up the hem of her caftan.

"Where did it get you, Brenda?"

She hardly recognized his shaken voice.

"My left leg," she whispered faintly. This was not how she had wanted him to find out.

She felt his hands on Ermatroid, releasing the velcro strap, pulling it away, removing the woolen stocking, exposing her withered, scarred stump to his gaze. Then urgent, doctorly hands were running over her leg, from the sensitive area around the scar, to her thigh.

"I think it must have rather battered fangs," Brenda heard the amused voice of Cathy say.

Brenda's eyes flew open and she was looking into such a gray, desperate face that she cried out.

As Cathy's words sank in, she saw tremendous relief fill his face.

"It bit her artificial leg. I forgot about her leg!" Blake didn't sound shocked. He wasn't looking with horror at her leg. Incredibly, she felt his hand slide over her leg, caressing it with relief, loving her.

"You knew?" Brenda asked.

The words were a mere whisper and, for a moment she thought he could not have heard as he stared at her uncomprehendingly, searching her face intently.

"Knew what?" Blake asked.

"About. . .about Ermatroid?

He stared blankly at her. Her heart plummeted. Then he looked helplessly at Jack.

"It's what she calls that necessary part of her," Jack said softly, nodding toward the discarded prosthesis.

Brenda looked from one loved face to the other. Some unspoken communication seemed to pass between the two men. Jack gave a brief nod.

Suddenly, fierce, black eyes were fastened on her face.

"Come on, you two youngsters. Show us where the kitchen is. Cath and I need a drink," she heard Jack say from a great distance. She thought vaguely that Rick tried to protest, but then there was nothing and no one to intrude between her and Blake's heart-stopping gaze.

Suddenly he yelled. "It. . .it was that wasn't it? All along it's been that. . .that damaged leg!" Blake said through clenched teeth.

Brenda hardly registered what his lips were saying. He had known, but he had forgotten! Suddenly it didn't matter one bit the when and the how. Whether his doctor's eyes had seen from the beginning. Whether he had felt it when he held her close to him. Whether Rick had told him. . .

"I love you. Just as you are. Ermatroid or no Ermatroid. Family or no family. Just you." Something must have flashed into her eyes. His expression changed. Despair again flooded his face, tightened his lips. "If you think I'm the type of low life that would think any the less of you because of your upbringing, I guess I have my answer. You can't really love me, after all."

His voice was shaking so much that she hardly recognized the usual deep tones that had thrilled her from that very first day. To her horror, tears filled those dark brown eyes, so filled with love. . .with longing. . .despair. . .

"Darling! Oh, darling Blake, don't look like that!" she cried desperately, reaching up to him, pulling him down to her, frantically trying to find his mouth with her own. "Of course I'll marry you. I love you desperately. I must have been mad, crazy. I couldn't live without you!"

For a moment his lips were cold and lifeless and then they sprang to burning life, taking. . .giving. . .

With God's love filling them both, sustaining them both, this dream would last forever, her heart sang.

And it did!

A Letter To Our Readers

Dear Reader:

In order that we might better contribute to your reading enjoyment, we would appreciate your taking a few minutes to respond to the following questions. When completed, please return to the following:

Rebecca Germany, Editor
Heartsong Presents
P.O. Box 719
Uhrichsville, Ohio 44683

1. Did you enjoy reading *Damaged Dreams*?
   ❑ Very much. I would like to see more books
     by this author!
   ❑ Moderately
     I would have enjoyed it more if _____

   _____

2. Are you a member of *Heartsong Presents*? Yes   No
   If no, where did you purchase this book? _____

   _____

3. What influenced your decision to purchase this
   book? (Check those that apply.)

   ❑ Cover   ❑ Back cover copy

   ❑ Title   ❑ Friends

   ❑ Publicity   ❑ Other _____

4. On a scale from 1 (poor) to 10 (superior), please rate the following elements.

___Heroine   ___Plot

___Hero   ___Inspirational theme

___Setting   ___Secondary characters

5. What settings would you like to see covered in *Heartsong Presents* books?

_____

_____

6. What are some inspirational themes you would like to see treated in future books?_____

_____

_____

7. Would you be interested in reading other *Heartsong Presents* titles?   ❏ Yes   ❏ No

8. Please check your age range:
❏ Under 18   ❏ 18-24   ❏ 25-34
❏ 35-45   ❏ 46-55   ❏ Over 55

9. How many hours per week do you read? _____

Name _____

Occupation _____

Address _____

City _____ State _____ Zip _____

Don't miss these favorite Heartsong Presents *titles by some of our most distinguished authors!*

Your price is only $2.95 each!

___HP01 A TORCH FOR TRINITY, *Colleen L. Reece*
___HP02 WILDFLOWER HARVEST, *Colleen L. Reece*
___HP03 RESTORE THE JOY, *Sara Mitchell*
___HP04 REFLECTIONS OF THE HEART, *Sally Laity*
___HP10 SONG OF LAUGHTER, *Lauraine Snelling*
___HP17 LLAMA LADY, *VeraLee Wiggins*
___HP18 ESCORT HOMEWARD, *Eileen M. Berger*
___HP19 A PLACE TO BELONG, *Janelle Jamison*
___HP23 GONE WEST, *Kathleen Karr*
___HP28 DAKOTA DAWN, *Lauraine Snelling*
___HP36 THE SURE PROMISE, *JoAnn A. Grote*
___HP39 GOVERNOR'S DAUGHTER, *Veda Boyd Jones*
___HP41 FIELDS OF SWEET CONTENT, *Norma Jean Lutz*
___HP42 SEARCH FOR TOMORROW, *Mary Hawkins*
___HP43 VEILED JOY, *Colleen L. Reece*
___HP44 DAKOTA DREAM, *Lauraine Snelling*

Send to: Heartsong Presents Reader's Service
P.O. Box 719
Uhrichsville, Ohio 44683

Please send me the items checked above. I am enclosing
$_____(please add $1.00 to cover postage and handling
per order. OH add 6.25% tax. NJ add 6% tax.).
Send check or money order, no cash or C.O.D.s, please.
To place a credit card order, call 1-800-847-8270.

NAME _____

ADDRESS _____

CITY/STATE _____ ZIP_____

FAVORITES

....Hearts ♥ng ....

Any 12 Heartsong Presents titles for only $26.95 *

···· Presents ··········

_HP 61 PICTURE PERFECT, *Susan Kirby*
_HP 62 A REAL AND PRECIOUS THING, *Brenda Bancroft*
_HP 65 ANGEL FACE, *Frances Carfi Matranga*
_HP 66 AUTUMN LOVE, *Ann Bell*
_HP 69 BETWEEN LOVE AND LOYALTY, *Susannah Hayden*
_HP 70 A NEW SONG, *Kathleen Yapp*
_HP 73 MIDSUMMER'S DREAM, *Rena Eastman*
_HP 74 SANTANONI SUNRISE, *Hope Irvin Marston and Claire M. Coughlin*
_HP 77 THE ROAD BEFORE ME, *Susannah Hayden*
_HP 78 A SIGN OF LOVE, *Veda Boyd Jones*
_HP 81 BETTER THAN FRIENDS, *Sally Laity*
_HP 82 SOUTHERN GENTLEMEN, *Yvonne Lehman*
_HP 85 LAMP IN DARKNESS, *Connie Loraine*
_HP 86 POCKETFUL OF LOVE, *Loree Lough*
_HP 89 CONTAGIOUS LOVE, *Ann Bell*
_HP 90 CATER TO A WHIM, *Norma Jean Lutz*
_HP 93 IDITAROD DREAM, *Janelle Jamison*
_HP 94 TO BE STRONG, *Carolyn R. Scheidies*
_HP 97 A MATCH MADE IN HEAVEN, *Kathleen Yapp*
_HP 98 BEAUTY FOR ASHES, *Becky Melby and Cathy Wienke*
_HP101 DAMAGED DREAMS, *Mary Hawkins*
_HP102 IF GIVEN A CHOICE, *Tracie J. Peterson*

Great Inspirational Romance at a Great Price!

Heartsong Presents books are inspirational romances in contemporary and historical settings, designed to give you an enjoyable, spirit-lifting reading experience. You can choose from 104 wonderfully written titles from some of today's best authors like Colleen L. Reece, Brenda Bancroft, Janelle Jamison, and many others.

When ordering quantities less than twelve, above titles are $2.95 each.

SEND TO: Heartsong Presents Reader's Service
P.O. Box 719, Uhrichsville, Ohio 44683

Please send me the items checked above. I am enclosing $ _____
(please add $1.00 to cover postage per order. OH add 6.25% tax. NJ
add 6%.). Send check or money order, no cash or C.O.D.s, please.
To place a credit card order, call 1-800-847-8270.

NAME _____

ADDRESS _____

CITY/STATE_____ ZIP _____

HPS DECEMBER

Heartsong Presents
Love Stories Are Rated G!

That's for godly, gratifying, and of course, great! If you love a thrilling love story, but don't appreciate the sordidness of popular paperback romances, **Heartsong Presents** is for you. In fact, **Heartsong Presents** is the *only inspirational romance book club*, the only one featuring love stories where Christian faith is the primary ingredient in a marriage relationship.

Sign up today to receive your first set of four, never before published Christian romances. Send no money now; you will receive a bill with the first shipment. You may cancel at any time without obligation, and if you aren't completely satisfied with any selection, you may return the books for an immediate refund!

Imagine. . .four new romances every month—two historical, two contemporary—with men and women like you who long to meet the one God has chosen as the love of their lives. . .all for the low price of $9.97 postpaid.

To join, simply complete the coupon below and mail to the address provided. **Heartsong Presents** romances are rated G for another reason: They'll arrive *Godspeed!*